A Demon in My View

All of the characters in this book
are fictitious, and any resemblance
to actual persons, living or dead,
is purely coincidental.

ISBN: 0-385-12110-5
Library of Congress Catalog Card Number 76-9486
Copyright © 1976 by Ruth Rendell
All Rights Reserved
Printed in the United States of America
First Edition in the United States of America

A Demon in My View

RUTH RENDELL

12 / 76 / Doubleday

DOUBLEDAY & COMPANY, INC.
GARDEN CITY, NEW YORK
1977

For Margaret Rabbs, with love

Author's Note

The Gunpowder Plot was an attempt to assassinate King James I of England and destroy the Houses of Lords and Commons on the day of the opening of Parliament, November 5, 1605. Fuel and explosives were concealed in a cellar under the House of Lords, but the conspirators were betrayed to the government before their design could be carried out. One of their number, Guy Fawkes, was arrested at midnight in the cellar doorway, brought to trial with his fellow conspirators and executed in January 1606.

Although Guy Fawkes met his death by hanging and not by burning at the stake, it has been a tradition with English children to commemorate November 5 by burning him in effigy each year on that date. This custom has never become "quaint" or mere ceremonial but is very much a part of English life.

From childhood's hour I have not been
As others were; I have not seen
As others saw; I could not bring
My passions from a common spring.
From the same source I have not taken
My sorrow; I could not awaken
My heart to joy at the same tone;
And all I loved, I loved alone.
Then—in my childhood, in the dawn
Of a most stormy life—was drawn
From every depth of good and ill
The mystery which binds me still . . .
And the cloud that took the form
(When the rest of Heaven was blue)
Of a demon in my view.

                              Edgar Allan Poe

A Demon in My View

The cellar was divided into rooms. Each of these caverns except the last of them was cluttered with the rubbish which usually encumbers the cellars of old houses: broken bicycles, old mould-grown leather cases, wooden crates, legless or armless chairs, cracked china vessels, yellowing newspapers bundled up with string, and in heaps, the nameless unidentifiable cylinders and tubes and rods and rings and spirals of metal which once, long ago, bolted or screwed or linked something on to something else. All this rubbish was coated with the thick black grime that is always present in cellars. The place smelt of soot and fungus.

Between the junk heaps a passage had been cleared from the steps to the first doorless doorway, on to the second doorway and thence to the bare room beyond. And in this room, unseen as yet in the pitch blackness, the figure of a woman leaned against the wall.

He came down the steps with a torch in his hand. He switched on the torch only when he had closed and bolted the door behind him. Then, led by its beam, he picked his way softly along the path that was hedged by rubbish. There was no sound but the shuffle of his slippers on the sooty stone, yet as he entered the second room he told himself he had heard ahead of him an indrawn breath, a small gasp of fear. He smiled, though he was trembling, and the hand which held the torch shook a little.

At the second doorway he raised the beam and let it play from the lower left-hand corner of the room upwards and then downwards, moving it languidly towards the right. It showed him pocked walls, a cracked ceiling hung with cobwebs. It showed him old, broken, long-disused electric wires, a trickle of viscous water running from the fissure in a split brick, and then, playing in a downward arc, it showed him the woman's figure.

Her white face, beautiful, unmarked by any flaw of skin or feature, stared blankly back at him. But he fancied, as the torch shivered in his hand, that she had cringed, her slim body in its short black dress pressing further into the wall which supported it. A handbag was hooked over one of her arms and she wore scuffed black shoes. He didn't speak. He had never known how to talk to women. There was only one thing he had ever been able to do to women and, advancing now, smiling, he did it.

First he rested the torch on a brick ledge at the level of his knees so that she was in shadow, so that the room took on the aspect of an alley into which a street lamp filters dimly. Then he approached her, paralysed as she was, and meeting no resistance —he would have preferred resistance—he closed his hands on her throat.

Still there was no resistance, but what happened next was almost as satisfactory. His hands squeezed till the fingers met, and as forefinger pressed against thumb, the beautiful white face changed, crumpled, twisted in agony and caved in. He gave a grunting gasp as her body fell sideways. He released his hold, swaying at the earthquake inside him, and he let her fall, prone and stiff, into the footmarked soot.

It took him a few minutes to recover. He wiped his hands and the corners of his mouth on a clean white handkerchief. He closed his eyes, opened them, sighed. Then he picked up the plastic shop window model and set her once more against the wall. Her face remained caved in. He wiped the dust from it with his handkerchief and, inserting his fingers through the split in her neck, a split which grew wider each time he murdered her, pushed out sunken nose and crumpled eyes and depressed chin, until she was blank and beautiful again.

He straightened her dress and replaced the handbag, which had come unhooked, once more on her arm. She was ready to die for him again. A week, a fortnight might go by, but she would wait for him. It was good, the best thing in his life, just knowing she was there, waiting till next time . . .

1

The houses were warrens for people, little anthills of discomfort. Almost each one, built to accommodate a single family, had been segmented into four or five separate units. Ungracious living was evinced by a row of doorbells, seven in an eight-roomed house, by the dustbins that had replaced rose bushes in the front gardens, by the slow decay that showed in a boarded window, a balcony rail patched with chicken wire, a latchless gate that tapped ceaselessly, monotonously, against its post.

On the odd-numbered side of Trinity Road the houses were tall and with high basements so that the flights of steps mounting to their front doors seemed to assault the very hearts of these houses like engines of siege. They faced terraces of brown brick, humbler-looking and only three floors high. Outside number 142 was parked a large shiny car, a green Jaguar. A toy dog that nodded its head at the slightest vibration rested inside the rear window, and hanging from the centre of the windscreen was a blond doll in a two-piece bathing suit.

The car looked incongruous in Trinity Road, along which such vehicles generally passed without stopping. Just inside the low wall that bounded the front garden of number 142 grew two lopped-off lime trees, stumps bearing on their summits excrescences of leathery leaves that gave them the look of prehistoric vegetation. Behind them was a small patch of brown turf. On the ground floor was a bay window, curtained in orange; above that two windows curtained in floral green—frayed curtains these, with a rent in one of them; on the top floor brown velvet curtains which, parted, disclosed a white frilly drapery like the bodice of a woman's nightgown.

A shallow flight of steps, of pink granite but grazed instead of polished, led to a front door whose woodwork might have been of any colour, green, brown, grey, it was so long since it had been painted. But the glass panels in it kept the dim glow they had always had, rubber plant green and the dull maroon of sour wine, the kind of stained glass found in chapel windows of the last century.

There were five bells, each one but the lowest labelled. A psychologist would have learned much from the varied and distinctive labelling of these bells. The topmost bore below it a typewritten slip, framed in a plastic container clearly designed for this purpose, which stated: Flat 2, Mr. A. Johnson. Beneath this and the next bell, on a scrap of card secured with adhesive tape, was scrawled in a bold reckless hand: Jonathan Dean. While under the third bell two labels seemed to quarrel with each other for pre-eminence. One was of brown plastic with the letters on it in relief: Flat 1, B. Kotowsky. Its rival, jostling it, stuck to the corner of it with a gob of glue, announced in felt-tipped pen: Ms. V. Kotowsky. Last came a frivolous oval of orange cardboard on which, under a pair of Chinese characters done with a brush, the caller might read: Room 1, Li-li Chan.

The space beneath the lowest bell was vacant as was Room 2 with which it communicated.

Between the door of the vacant room and the long diagonal sweep which was the underside of the staircase, a shabby windowless space, Stanley Caspian, the landlord, had his office. It was furnished with a desk and two bentwood chairs. On top of the shelves, bristling with papers, which lined the rear wall, stood an electric kettle and a couple of cups and saucers. There was no other furniture in the hall but a rectangular mahogany table set against the banisters and facing the ground floor bathroom.

Stanley Caspian sat at the desk, as he always did when he came to 142 for his Saturday morning conference with Arthur

Johnson. Arthur sat in the other chair. On the desk were spread the rent books and cheques of the tenants. Each rent book had its own brown envelope with the tenant's name printed on it. This had been an innovation of Arthur's and he had done the printing. Stanley wrote laboriously in the rent books, pressing his pen in hard and making unnecessary full-stops after every word and figure.

"I'll be glad to see the back of that Dean," he said when he had inked in the last fifty pence and made the last full-stop. "Middle of next month and he'll be gone."

"And his gramophone," said Arthur, "and his wine bottles filling up our little dustbin. I'm sure we'll all be devoutly thankful."

"Not Kotowsky. He won't have anyone to go boozing with. Still, thank God he's going off his own bat, is what I say. I'd never have been able to get rid of him, not with this poxy new Rent Act. Put the kettle on, me old Arthur. I fancy a spot of elevenses."

And tenses and twelveses, Arthur thought. He plugged in the electric kettle and set out the cups. He wouldn't have dreamed of eating anything at this hour, but Stanley, who was enormously fat, whose belly almost burst open the front of his size-seventeen-collar shirt, opened one of the packages he had brought with him and began devouring sandwiches of bread rolls and processed cheese. Stanley spluttered crumbs all over his shirt, eating uninhibitedly like some gross, superannuated baby. Arthur watched him inscrutably. He neither liked nor disliked Stanley. For him, as for everyone, he had no particular feeling most of the time. He wished only to be esteemed, to keep in with the right people, to know where he stood. Inclining his head towards the door behind him, he said:

"A little bird told me you'd let that room."

"Right," said Stanley, his mouth full. "A little Chinese bird, was it?"

"I must confess I was a bit put out you told Miss Chan before telling me. You know me, I always believe in speaking out. And I was a little hurt. After all, I am your oldest tenant. I *have* been here twenty years, and I think I can say I've never caused you a moment's unease."

"Right. I only wish they were all like you."

Arthur filled the cups with instant coffee, boiling water and a dribble of cold milk. "No doubt, you had your reasons." He lifted cold eyes, of so pale a blue as to be almost white. "I mustn't be so sensitive."

"The fact is," said Stanley, shovelling spoonfuls of sugar into his cup, "that I wondered how you'd take it. You see, this new chap, the one that's taking Room 2, he's got the same name as you." He gave Arthur a sidelong look and then he chortled. "You have to laugh. Coincidence, eh? I wondered how you'd take it."

"You mean he's also called *Arthur Johnson?*"

"Not so bad as that. Dear oh dear, you have to laugh. He's called Anthony Johnson. You'll have to take care your post doesn't get mixed up. Don't want him reading your love letters, eh?"

Arthur's eyes seemed to grow even paler, and the muscles of his face tightened, tensed, drawing it into a mask. When he spoke his accent smoothed into an exquisite, slightly affected English. "I've nothing to hide. My life is an open book."

"Maybe his isn't. If I wasn't in a responsible position I'd say you could have a bit of fun there, me old Arthur." Stanley finished his sandwiches and fetched a doughnut from the second bag. "*Sexual Behavior in the Human Male*, that's the sort of open book his life'll be. Good-looking young devil, he is. Real flypaper for the girls, I shouldn't wonder."

Arthur couldn't bear that sort of talk. It made him feel sick. "I only hope he's got a good bank reference and a decent job."

"Right. He's paid two months' rent in advance and that's better than all your poxy bank references to me. He's moving in Monday." Stanley got heavily to his feet. Crumbs cascaded onto desk, envelopes, and rent books. "We'll just have a look in, Arthur. Mrs. Caspian says there's a fruit bowl in there she wants and young Anthony'll only smash it."

Arthur nodded sagely. If he and his landlord were in agreement about anything, it was the generally destructive behaviour of the other tenants. Besides, he enjoyed penetrating the rooms, usually closed to him. And in this one he had a special interest.

It was small and furnished with junk. Arthur accepted this as proper in a furnished room, noting only that it was far from clean. He picked his way over to the window. Stanley, having secured his fruit bowl, of red and white Venetian glass, from heterogeneous stacks of crockery and cutlery on the draining board, was admiring the only object in the place less than twenty years old.

"That's a bloody good washbasin, that is," he remarked, tapping this article of primrose-coloured porcelain. "Cost me all of fifteen quid to have that put in. Your people did it, as I remember."

"It was a reject," said Arthur absently. "There's a flaw in the soap dish." He was staring out of the window which overlooked a narrow brick-walled court. Above an angle of wall you could see the topmost branches of a tree. The court was concreted and the concrete was green with lichen, for into the two drains on either side of it flowed—and sometimes overflowed—the waste water from the two upstairs flats and Jonathan Dean's room. In the wall which faced the window was a door.

"What are you looking at?" said Stanley, none too pleasantly, for Arthur's remark about the washbasin had perhaps rankled.

"Nothing," said Arthur. "I was just thinking he won't have much of an outlook."

"What d'you expect for seven quid a week? You want to remember *you* pay seven for a whole flat because the poxy government won't let me charge more for unfurnished accommodation. You're lucky, getting your hooks on that when I didn't know any better. Oh yes. But times have changed, thank God, and for seven quid a week now you look out on a cellar door and lump it. Right?"

"It's no concern of mine," said Arthur. "I imagine my namesake will be out a lot, won't he?"

"If he's got any sense," said Stanley, for at that moment there crashed through the ceiling the triumphant chords of the third movement from Beethoven's Eighth. "Tschaikowsky," he said learnedly. "Dean's at it again. I like something a bit more modern myself."

"I was never musical." Arthur gravitated into the hall. "I must get on with things. Shopping day, you know. If I might just have my little envelope?"

~~~~~~~~~

His shopping basket in one hand and an orange plastic carrier containing his laundry in the other, Arthur made his way along Trinity Road towards the launderette in Brasenose Avenue. He could have used the Coinerama in Magdalen Hill, but he went to Magdalen Hill every weekday to work and at the weekends he liked to vary his itinerary. After all, for good reason, he didn't go out much and never after dark.

So instead of cutting through Oriel Mews, past the Waterlily pub and making for the crossroads, he went down past All Souls' Church, where as a child he had passed two hours each Sabbath Day, his text carefully committed to memory. And at four o'clock Auntie Gracie had always been waiting for him, always, it seemed to him, under an umbrella. Had it invariably rained on Sundays, the granite terrace opposite veiled in misty grey? That terrace was now gone, replaced by barracklike blocks of council flats.

He followed the route he and Auntie Gracie had taken towards home, but only for a little way. Taking some pleasure in making the K.12 bus stop for him alone, Arthur went over the pedestrian crossing in Balliol Street, holding up his hand in an admonitory way. Down St. John's Road, where the old houses still remained, turn-of-the-century houses some enterprising but misguided builder had designed with Dutch façades, and where plane trees alternated with concrete lamp standards.

The launderette attendant said, "Good morning," and Arthur rejoined with a cool nod. He used his own soap in the machine. He didn't trust the blue stuff in the little packet you got for five-pence. Nor did he trust the attendant to put his linen in the drier nor the other customers not to steal it. So he sat patiently on one of the benches, talking to no one, until the thirty-five-minute cycle was completed.

It afforded him considerable satisfaction to note how superior were his pale blue sheets, snowy towels, underwear and shirts, to the gaudy jumble sale laundry in the adjacent machines. While they were safely rotating in the drier, he went next door to the butcher's and then to the greengrocer's. Arthur never shopped in the supermarkets run by Indians, in which this area of Kenbourne Vale abounded. He selected his lamb chops, his small Sunday joint of Scotch topside, with care. Three slices off the roast for Sunday, the rest to be minced and made into Monday's cottage pie. A pound of runner beans, and pick out the small ones, if you please, he didn't want a mouthful of strings.

A different way back. The linen so precisely folded that it wouldn't really need ironing—though Arthur always ironed it— he trotted up Merton Street. More council flats, tower blocks here like pillars supporting the heavy, overcast sky. The lawns which separated them, Arthur had often noticed with satisfaction, were prohibited to children. The children played in the street or sat disconsolately on top of bits of sculpture. Arthur disapproved of the sculptures, which in his view resembled chunks cut out of prehistoric monsters for all they were entitled "Spring" or "Social Conscience" or "Man and Woman," but he didn't think the children ought to sit on them or play in the street for that matter. Auntie Gracie had never allowed him to play in the street.

Stanley Caspian's Jaguar had gone, and so had the Kotowskys' fourth-hand Ford. A fistful of vouchers, entitling their possessor to threepence off toothpaste or free soap when you bought a giant size shampoo, had been pushed through the letter box. Arthur helped himself to those which might come in handy, and mounted the stairs. There was a half-landing after the ten steps of the first flight where a pay phone box was attached to the wall. Four steps went on to the first floor. The door of the Kotowskys' flat was on his left, that to Jonathan Dean's room facing him, and the door to the bathroom they shared between the other two. Dean's door was open, Shostakovitch's Fifth Symphony on loud enough to be heard in Kenbourne Town Hall. The intention apparently was that it should be loud enough merely to be audible in the bathroom from which Dean, a tall, red-haired, red-faced man now emerged. He wore nothing but a small mauve towel fastened round him loincloth-fashion.

"The body is more than raiment," he remarked when he saw Arthur.

Arthur flushed slightly. It was his belief that Dean was mad, a conviction which rested partly on the fact that everything the man said sounded as if it had come out of a book. He turned his head in the direction of the open door.

"Would you be good enough to reduce the volume a little, Mr. Dean?"

Dean said something about music having charms to soothe the savage breast, and beat his own, which was hairy and covered with freckles. But, having slammed his door with violence but no animosity, he subdued Shostakovitch and only vague Slavic murmurs reached Arthur as he ascended the second flight.

And now he was in his own exclusive domain. He occupied the whole second floor. With a sigh of contentment, resting his laundry bag and his shopping basket on the mat, he unlocked the door and let himself in.

2

Arthur prepared his lunch, two lamb cutlets, creamed potatoes, runner beans. None of your frozen or canned rubbish for him. Auntie Gracie had brought him up to appreciate fresh food, well-cooked. He ended the meal with a slice from the plum pie he had baked on Thursday night, and then, without delay, he washed the dishes. One of Auntie Gracie's maxims had been that only slatternly housekeepers leave dirty dishes in the sink. Arthur always washed his the moment he finished eating.

He went into the bedroom. The bed was stripped. He put on clean sheets, rose pink, and rose pink pillowcases. Arthur couldn't sleep in a soiled bed. Once, when collecting their rent, he had caught a glimpse of the Kotowskys' bed and it had put him off his supper.

Meticulously he dusted the bedroom furniture and polished the silver stoppers on Auntie Gracie's cut-glass scent bottles. All his furniture was late Victorian, pretty though a little heavy. It came up well under an application of polish. Arthur still felt guilty about using spray-on polish instead of the old-fashioned wax kind. Auntie Gracie had never approved of short cuts. He gave the frilly nets with which every window in the flat was curtained a critical stare. They were too fragile to be risked at the launderette, so he washed them himself once a month, and they weren't due for a wash for another week. But this was such a grimy district, and there was nothing like white net for collecting every bit of flying dust. He began to take them down. For the second time that day he found himself facing the cellar door.

The Kotowskys had no window which overlooked it. It could

be seen only from this one of his and from the one in Room 2. This had long been known to Arthur, he had known it for nearly as long as the duration of his tenancy. Very little in his own life had changed in those twenty years. The cellar door had never been painted, though the bricks had darkened perhaps and the concrete grown more green and damp. No one had ever seen him cross that yard, he thought as he laid the net curtains carefully over a chair, no one had ever seen him enter the cellar. He continued to stare down, considering, remembering.

He had been at school with Stanley Caspian—Merton Street Junior—and Stanley had been fat and gross and coarse even then. A bully always.

"Auntie's baby! Auntie's baby! Where's your dad, Arthur Johnson?" And with an inventiveness no one would have suspected from the standard of Stanley's school work: "Cowardy, cowardy custard, Johnson is a bastard!"

The years civilise or, at least, inhibit. When they met by chance in Trinity Road, each aged thirty-two, Stanley was affable, even considerate.

"Sorry to hear you lost your aunt, Arthur. More like a mother to you, she was."

"Yes."

"You'll be wanting a place of your own now. Bachelor flat, eh? How about taking the top of a hundred and forty-two?"

"I've no objection to giving it the once-over," said Arthur primly. He knew old Mrs. Caspian had left her son a lot of property in West Kenbourne.

The house was in a mess in those days and the top flat was horrible. But Arthur saw its potential—and for two pounds ten a week?

So he took Stanley's offer, and a couple of days later when he had started the redecorating he went down into the cellar to see if, by chance, it housed a stepladder.

She was lying on the floor of the furthest room on a heap of sacks and black-out curtains left over from the war. She was naked and her white plastic flesh was cold and shiny. He never found out who had brought her there and left her entombed. At first he had been embarrassed, taken aback as he was when he glimpsed likenesses of her standing in shop windows and waiting to be dressed. But then, because he was alone with her and there was no one to see them, he approached more closely. So that was how they looked? With awe, with fear, at last with distaste, he looked at the two hemispheres on her chest, the soft, swollen triangle between her closed thighs. An impulse came to him to dress her. He had done so many secret things in his life—almost everything he had done that he had wanted to do had been covert, clandestine—that no inhibition intervened to stop him fetching from the flat a black dress, a handbag, shoes. These had belonged to Auntie Gracie and he had brought them with him from the house in Magdalen Hill. People had suggested he give them to the WVS for distribution, but how could he? How could he have borne to see some West Kenbourne slattern queening it in her clothes?

His white lady had attenuated limbs and was as tall as he. Auntie Gracie's dress came above her knees. She had yellow nylon hair that curled over her cheekbones. He put the shoes on her feet and hooked the handbag over her arm. In order to see what he was doing, he had put a hundred-watt bulb in the light socket. But another of those impulses led him to take it out. By the light of the torch she looked real, the cellar room with its raw brick walls an alley in the hinterland of city streets. It was sacrilege to dress her in Auntie Gracie's clothes, and yet that very sacrilege had an indefinable rightness about it, was a spur. . . .

He had strangled her before he knew what he was doing. With his bare hands on her cold smooth throat. The release had been almost as good as the real thing. He set her up against the wall once more, dusted her beautiful white face. You do not have to hide or fear or sweat for such a killing; the law permits you to kill anything not made of flesh and blood. . . . He left her and came out into the yard. The room that was now Room 2 had been untenanted then as had the whole house but for his flat. And when a tenant had come he had been, as had his successor, on night work that took him out five evenings a week at six. But before that Arthur had decided. She should save him, she should be—as those who would like to get hold of him would call it—his therapy. The women who waited in the dark streets, asking for trouble, he cared nothing for them, their pain, their terror. He cared, though, for his own fate. To defy it, he would kill a thousand women in her person, she should be his salvation. And then no threat could disturb him, provided he was careful never to go out after dark, never to have a drink.

After a time he had come to be rather proud of his solution. It seemed to set down as nonsense the theories of those experts—he had, in the days of his distress, studied their works—that men with his problem had no self-control, no discipline over their own compulsions. He had always known they talked rubbish. Why shouldn't he have the recourse of the members of Alcoholics Anonymous, of the rehabilitated drug addict?

But now? Anthony Johnson. Arthur, who made it his business to know the routines and lifestyles of his fellow tenants, hoped he would soon acquire a thoroughgoing knowledge of the new man's movements. Anthony Johnson would surely go out two or three evenings a week? He must. The alternative was something Arthur didn't at all want to face.

There was nothing for it but to wait and see. The possibility of bringing the white lady up into the flat, installing her here, killing her here, occurred to him only for him to dismiss the idea. He disliked the notion of his encounters with her taking on the air of a game. It was the squalor of the cellar, the dimness, his stealthy approach that gave to it its reality. No, she must remain there, he thought, and he must wait and see. He turned from the window and at the same time turned his mind, for he didn't much care to dwell upon her and what she truly was, preferring her to stand down there forgotten and unacknowledged until he needed her again. This, in fact, he thought as he took away the curtains to put them in soak, was the first time he had thought of her in those terms for many years.

Dismissing her as a man dismisses a compliant and always available mistress, Arthur went into the living room. The sofa and the two armchairs had been reupholstered since Auntie Gracie's death, only six months after, but Arthur had taken such good care of them that the covers still looked new. Carefully he worked on the blue moquette with a stiff brush. The cream drawn-thread antimacassars might as well go into the water with the nets. He polished the oval mahogany table, the mahogany tallboy, the legs and arms of the dining chairs; plumped up the blue and brown satin cushions, flicked his feather duster over the two hand-painted parchment lampshades, the knobs on the television set, the Chelsea china in the cabinet. Now for the vacuum cleaner. Having the flat entirely covered with wall-to-wall carpet in a deep fawn shade had made a hole in his savings, but it had been worth it. He ran the cleaner slowly and thoroughly over every inch of the carpet, taking his time so that its droning zoom-zoom wouldn't be lost on Jonathan Dean, though he had little hope of its setting him an example. Finally, he rinsed the nets and the chair backs and hung them over the drying rack in the bathroom. There was no need to clean the bathroom or the kitchen. They were cleaned every morning as a matter of course, the former when he had dried himself after his bath, the latter as soon as breakfast was over.

At this point he sat down in the chair by the front window and, having left all his doors open, surveyed the flat along its spotless length. It smelt of polish, silver cleaner, soap, and elbow grease. Arthur recalled how, when he was about eleven and had neglected to wash his bedroom window as thoroughly as Auntie Gracie demanded, she had sent him round to Winter's with threepence.

"You ask the man for a pound of elbow grease, Arthur. Go on. It won't take you five minutes."

The man in the shop had laughed himself almost into a fit. But he hadn't explained why he had no elbow grease, and Arthur had to take the threepenny bit—a threepenny joey, they called them then—back home again.

"I expect he did laugh," said Auntie Gracie. "And I hope you've been taught a lesson." She rubbed Arthur's arm through the grey flannel shirt. "This is where your elbow grease comes from. You can't buy it, you have to make it yourself."

Arthur hadn't borne her any malice. He knew she had acted for the best. He would do exactly the same by any child in his charge. Children had to be taught the hard way, and it had set him on the right path. Would she be pleased with him if she could see him now? If she could see how well he kept his own place, his bank balance, how he ordered his life, how he hadn't missed a day at Grainger's in twenty years? Perhaps. But she had never been very pleased with him, had she? He had never reached those heights of perfection she had laid before him as fitting for one who needed to cleanse himself of the taint of his birth and background.

Arthur sighed. He should have washed the Chelsea china. It was no good telling himself a flick with that duster would serve as well as a wash. Tired now but determined to soldier on, he put the shepherdesses and frock-coated gentlemen and dogs and little flower baskets onto a tray and carried them into the kitchen.

3

Arthur was a sound sleeper. He fell asleep within five minutes of laying his head on the pillow and hardly ever awoke before the alarm went off at seven-thirty. This ability to sleep was something to confound those silent critics, that invisible army of psychiatrists whose words he had read but never yet heard, and who would, he suspected, categorise him disagreeably. Which was absurd. Neurotic people don't sleep well, nor do hysterics. Arthur knew he was a perfectly normal man who happened (like all normal men) to have a small peculiarity he was well able to keep under control.

He was always the last to leave for work and the first to get home. This was because the others all worked further afield than he. Jonathan Dean went first. He left at five past eight while Arthur was still in his bath. This Monday morning his room door was slammed so loudly that the bath water actually rocked about like tea in a joggled cup. The front door also crashed shut. Arthur dried himself and, for decency's sake, put on his towelling robe before washing down bath, basin, and floor. As soon as he was dressed, he opened his own front door and left it on the latch.

The Kotowskys burst out of their flat while he was pouring out his cornflakes. As usual, they were quarrelling.

"All right, I get the message," he heard Brian Kotowsky say. "You've told me three times you won't be in tonight."

"I just don't want you ringing up all my friends, asking where I am."

"You can settle that one, Vesta, by telling me where you'll be."

They clumped down the stairs, still arguing, but Arthur couldn't catch Vesta Kotowsky's reply. The front door closed fairly quietly which meant Vesta must have shut it. Arthur went to his living room window and watched them get into their car which was left day in and day out, rain, shine or snow, parked in the street. He was sincerely glad he had never taken the step of getting married, had, in fact, taken such a serious step to avoid it.

As he was returning to his kitchen he heard Li-li Chan come upstairs to the half-landing and the phone. Li-li spoke quite good English but rather as a talking bird might have spoken it. Her voice was high and clipped. She was always giggling, mostly about nothing.

She giggled now, into the receiver. "You pick me up soon? Quarter to nine? Oh, you are nice, nice man. Do I love you? I don't know. Yes, yes, I love you. I love lots, lots of people. Good-bye now." Li-li giggled prettily all the way back down the stairs.

Arthur snorted, but not loudly enough for her to hear. London Transport wouldn't get rich out of her. Don't suppose she ever spends a penny on a train or bus fare, Arthur thought, and darkly, I wonder what she has to do to make it worth their while? But he didn't care to pursue that one, it was too distasteful.

He heard her go out on the dot of a quarter to. She always closed the doors very softly as if she had something to hide. A well-set-up, clean-looking young Englishman had come for her in a red sports car. A wicked shame, Arthur thought, but boys like that had only themselves to blame, they didn't know the meaning of self-discipline.

Alone in the house now, he finished his breakfast, washed the dishes, and wiped down all the surfaces. The post was due at nine. While he was brushing the jacket of his second-best suit and selecting a tie, he heard the dull thump of the letter box. Arthur always took the post in and arranged the letters on the hall table.

But first there was his rubbish to deal with. He lifted the liner from the wastebin, secured the top of it with a wire fastener and went downstairs, first making sure, with a quick glance into the mirror, that his tie was neatly knotted and that there was a clean

white handkerchief in his breast pocket. Whether there was anyone in the house or not, Arthur would never have gone downstairs improperly dressed. Nor would he set foot outside the
house without locking the doors behind him, not even to go to the
dustbin. Once more, the bin was choked with yellowish decay-
ing bean sprouts, not even wrapped up. That wasteful Li-li
again! He would have to make it clear to Stanley Caspian that
one dustbin was inadequate for five people—six, when this new
man came today.

Unlocking the door and re-entering the house, he picked up
the post. The usual weekly letter, postmarked Taiwan, from Li-
li's father who hadn't adopted Western ways and wrote the
sender's name as Chan Ah Feng. Poor trusting man, thought
Arthur, little did he know. Yet another bill for Jonathan Dean.
The next thing they'd have debt collectors round, and a fine
thing that would be for the house's reputation. Two letters for
the Kotowskys, one for her and one for both of them. That was
the way it always was.

He tidied up the circulars and vouchers—who messed them
about like that out of sheer wantonness he didn't know—and
then he arranged the letters, their envelope edges aligned to
each other and the edge of the table. Ten past nine. Sighing a
little, because it was so pleasant having the house to himself,
Arthur went back upstairs and collected his briefcase. He had no
real need of a briefcase for he never brought work home, but
Auntie Gracie had given him his first one for his twenty-first
birthday and since then he had replaced it three times. Besides,
it looked well. Auntie Gracie had always said that a man going
to business without a briefcase is as ill dressed as a lady without
gloves.

He closed his door and tested it with his hand to make sure it
was fast shut. Down the stairs once more and out into Trinity
Road. A fine, bright day, though somewhat autumnal. What else
could you expect in late September?

Grainger's, Contractors and Builders' Merchants, weren't due
to open until nine-thirty, and Arthur was early. He lingered to
look at the house where he had lived with Auntie Gracie. It was
on the corner of Balliol Street and Magdalen Hill, at the point
where the hill became Kenbourne Lane, a tall narrow house,

condemned to demolition but still waiting along with its neighbours to be demolished. The front door and the downstairs bay
were sealed up with gleaming silvery corrugated iron to stop
squatters and other vagrants from getting in. Arthur often wondered what Auntie Gracie would say if she could see it now, but
he approved of the sealing up. He paused at the gate and looked
up to the boarded rectangle on the brick façade which had once
been his bedroom window.

Auntie Gracie had been very good to him. He could never
make up to her for what she had done for him if he struggled till
the day of his death. He knew well what she had done, for, apart
from the concrete evidence of it all around him, she had never
missed an opportunity of telling him.

"After all I've done for you, Arthur!"

She had bought him from his mother, her own sister, when he
was two months old.

"Had to give her a hundred pounds, Arthur, and a hundred
was a lot of money in those days. We never saw her again. She
was off like greased lightning."

How fond Auntie Gracie had been of grease! Elbow grease,
greased lightning—"You need a bit of grease under your heels,
Arthur."

She had told him the facts of his birth as soon as she thought
him old enough to understand. Unfortunately, Stanley Caspian
and others of his ilk had thought him old enough some months
before, but that was no fault of hers. And she had never mentioned his mother or his father, whoever he may have been, at
all. But in that bedroom—with the door open, of course. She
insisted on his always leaving the door open—he had spent many
childhood hours, wondering. How foolish children were and how
ungrateful. . . .

Arthur shook himself and gave a slight cough. People would
be looking at him in a moment. He deplored anything that might
attract attention to oneself. And why on earth had he been
mooning away like this when he passed the house every day,
when there had been no unusual circumstance to give rise to
such a reverie? But, of course, there was an unusual circumstance. The new man was coming to Room 2. It was only natural
that today he should dwell a little on his past life. Natural, but

governable too. He turned briskly away from the gate as All
Souls' clock struck the half-hour. Grainger's yard was next door
but one to the sealed-up house, next to that a half-acre or so of
waste ground where houses had been demolished but not yet
replaced; beyond that Kenbourne Lane tube station.

Arthur unlocked the double gates and let himself into the glass
and cedarwood hut which was his office. The boy who made tea
and swept up and ran errands and whose duty it was to open the
place hadn't yet arrived. Typical. He wouldn't be late like this
morning after morning if he had had an Auntie Gracie to put a
spot of grease under his heels.

Raising the venetian blinds to let sunshine into the small, neat
room, Arthur took the cover off his Adler standard. Plenty of
post had come since Friday, mostly returned bills with cheques
enclosed. There was one irate letter from a customer who said
that a pastel blue sink unit had been installed by Grainger's in
his kitchen instead of the stainless steel variety he had ordered.
Arthur read it carefully, planning what diplomatic words he
would write in reply.

He called himself, when required to state his occupation, a
surveyor. In fact, he had never surveyed anything and wouldn't
have known how to go about it. His work consisted simply in sitting at this desk from nine-thirty till five, answering the phone,
sending out bills and keeping the books. He knew his work back
to front, inside out, but it still caused him anxiety, for Auntie
Gracie's standards were always before him.

"Never put off till tomorrow what you can do today, Arthur.
Remember if a job's worth doing, it's worth doing well. Your em-
ployer has reposed his trust in you. He has put you in a responsible position and it's up to you not to let him down."

Those, or words like them, had been the words with which she
had sent him off to be Grainger's boy a week after his fourteenth
birthday. So he had swept up better than anyone else and made
tea better than anyone else. When he was twenty-one he had at-
tained his present responsibility, that of seeing to it that every
customer of Grainger's got his roof mended better than anyone
else's roof and his kitchen floor laid better than anyone else's
kitchen floor. And he had seen to it. He was invaluable.

Dear Sir, Arthur typed, *I note with regret that the Rosebud de Luxe sink unit (type E/4283, pastel blue) was not, in fact*

Barry Hopkins slouched into the office, chewing bubble gum. "Hi."

"Good morning, Barry. A little late, aren't you? Do you know what time it is?"

"Round half nine," said Barry.

"I see. Round half nine. Of all the lackadaisical, feckless . . ." Arthur would have liked to advise him to go over to the works and ask for a pound of elbow grease, but the young were so sophisticated these days. Instead he snapped, "Take that filthy stuff out of your mouth."

Barry took no notice. He blew an enormous bubble, like a balloon and of a pale shade of aquamarine. Leaning idly on the window sill, he said:

"Old Grainger's comin' across the yard."

Arthur was galvanised. He composed his face into an expression suggestive of a mixture of devotion to duty, self-esteem and simpering sycophancy, and applied his hands to the typewriter.

4

Anthony Johnson had no furniture. He possessed nothing but a few clothes and a lot of books. These he had brought with him to 142 Trinity Road in a large old suitcase and a canvas bag. There were works on sociology, psychology, his dictionary of psychology, and that essential textbook for any student of the subject, *The Psychopath*, by William and Joan McCord. Whatever else he needed for reference he would obtain from the British Museum, and from that excellent library of criminology—the best, it was said, in London—housed in Radclyffe College, Kenbourne Vale. In that library too he would write the thesis whose subject was "Some Aspects of the Psychopathic Personality," and which he hoped would secure him from the University of London his doctorate of philosophy.

Part of it, he thought, surveying Room 2, would have to be written here. In that fireside chair, presumably, which seemed to be patched with bits from a woman's tweed skirt. On that crippled gate-leg table. Under that hanging lamp that looked like a monstrous joke-shop plastic jellyfish. Well, he wanted his Ph.D and this was the price he must pay for it. Dr. Johnson. Not, of course, that he would call himself doctor. It was Helen who had pointed out that in this country, the land of such anomalies, the bachelor of medicine is called doctor and the doctor of philosophy mister. She too had seen the funny side of being Dr. Johnson and had quoted epigrams and talked about Boswell until he, at last, had seen the point. But it was always so. Sometimes he thought that for all his Cambridge First, his Home Office Social Science diploma, his wide experience of working with the poor,

the sick and the deprived, he had never woken up to awareness
and insight until he met Helen. She it was who had turned his
soul's eye towards the light.

But as he thought this, he turned his physical eye towards
Stanley Caspian's green-spotted fingermarked mirror and surveyed his own reflection. He wasn't a vain man. He hardly ever
thought about the way he looked. That he was tall and slim and
strongly made with straight features and thick fair hair had
never meant much to him except in that they denoted health.
But lately he had come to wonder. He wondered what he lacked
that Roger had; he who was good-looking and vigorous and—
well, good company, wasn't he?—hypereducated with a good sal-
ary potential, and Roger, who was stupid and dull and posses-
sive and couldn't do anything but win pistol-shooting contests.
Only he knew it wasn't that at all. It was just that Helen, for all
her awareness, didn't know her own mind.

To give her a chance to know it, to choose between them, he
had come here. The library, of course, was an advantage. But he
could easily have written his thesis in Bristol. The theory was
that absence made the heart grow fonder. If he had gone to his
parents in York she could have phoned him every night. He
wasn't going to let her know the phone number here—he didn't
know it himself yet—or communicate with her at all except on
the last Wednesday in the month when Roger would be out at
his gun club. And he couldn't write to her at all in case Roger in-
tercepted the letter. She'd write to him once a week. He wondered, as he unpacked his books, how that would work out, if he
had been wise to let her call the tune, make all the arrangements. Well, he'd given her a deadline. By November she must
know. Stay in prison or come out with him into the free air.

He opened the window because the room smelt stale. Outside
was a narrow yard. What light it received came from a bit of sky
just flicked at its edges by leaves from a distant tree. The sky
was a triangular patch because most of it was cut off by brick
wall meeting brick wall diagonally about four yards up. In one
of these walls—they were festooned with pipes betwigged with
smaller pipes like lianas—was a door. Since there was no window
beside it or above it or anywhere near it, Anthony decided it
must lead down to a cellar.

Five o'clock. He had better go out and get himself something to cook on that very old and inefficient-looking Baby Belling stove. The hall smelt vaguely of cloves, less vaguely of old, unwashed fabrics. That would be the bathroom, that door between his and Room 1, and that other one to the right of old Caspian's table, the loo. Wondering what sort of a woman or girl Miss Chan was and whether she would get possession of the bathroom just when he wanted to use it, he went out into the street.

Trinity Road. It led him via Oriel Mews into Balliol Street. The street names of London, he thought, require an historical treatise of their own. Someone must know why this group in Hampstead are called after Devon towns and that cluster in Cricklewood after Hebridean islands. Were the Barbara, the Dorinda and the Lesly, after whom roads are named just north of the City, once the belles of Barnsbury? Did a sorcerer live in Warlock Road, Kilburn Park, and who was the Sylvia of Sylvia Gardens, Wembley, what is she, that all our maps commend her? In that corner of Kenbourne Vale, to which his destiny had drawn Anthony Johnson, someone had christened the squalid groves and terraces after Oxford colleges.

A cruel joke cannot have been intended. The councillor or town planner or builder must have thought himself inspired when he named Trinity Road, All Souls Grove, Magdalen Hill, Brasenose Avenue, and Wadham Street. What was certain, Anthony thought, was that he hadn't been an Oxford man, had never walked in the enclosed quadrangles of that city or even seen its dreaming spires.

Such a fanciful reverie would once have been alien to him. Helen had taught him to think like this, to see through her eyes, to associate, to compare, and to dream. She was all imagination, he all practical. Practical again, he noted mundane things. The Vale Café for quick, cheap snacks; Kemal's Kebab House, smelling of cumin and sesame and fenugreek, for when he wanted to splash a bit; a pub—the Waterlily, it was called. Just opening now. Anthony saw red plush settees, a brown-painted moulded ceiling, etched glass screens beside and behind the bar.

The pavements everywhere were cluttered with garbage in black plastic sacks. A dustmen's strike, perhaps. The kids were out of school. He wondered where they played. Always on these dusty pavements of Portland stone? Or on that bit of waste ground, fenced in with broken and rusty tennis court wire, between Grainger's, the builders, and the tube station?

Houses marked here for demolition. The sooner they came down the better and made way for flats with big windows and green spaces to surround them. Not many truly English people about. Brown women pushing prams with black babies in them, gypsy-looking women with hard, worn faces, Indian women with Marks and Spencers woolly cardigans over lilac and gold and turquoise saris. Cars parked everywhere, and vans double-parked on a street that was littered with torn paper and bruised vegetables and silvery fish scales where a market had just packed up and gone. Half-past five. But very likely that corner shop, Winter's, stayed open till all hours. He went in, bought a packet of ham, a can of beans, some bread, eggs, tea, margarine, and frozen peas. Carried along by a tide of home-going commuters, he returned to 142 Trinity Road. The house was no longer empty.

~~~~~~~~~

A man of about fifty was standing by the hall table, holding in his hand a bundle of cheap offer vouchers. He was tallish, thin, with a thin, reddish and coarse-skinned face. His thin, greyish-fair hair had been carefully combed to conceal a bald patch and was flattened with Brylcreem. He wore an immaculate dark grey suit, a white shirt, and a maroon tie dotted with tiny silver spots. On his rather long, straight, and quite fleshless nose, were a pair of gold-rimmed glasses. When he saw Anthony he jumped.

"These were on the mat," he said. "They come every day. You wouldn't think there was a world paper shortage, would you? I tidy them up. No one else seems to be interested. But I hardly feel it's my place to throw them away."

Anthony wondered why he bothered to explain.

"I'm Anthony Johnson," he said. "I moved in today."

The man said, "Ah," and held out his hand. He had a rather donnish look as if he perhaps had been responsible for the naming of those streets. But his voice was uneducated, underlying the pedantic preciseness Kenbourne Vale's particular brand of cockney. "Moved into the little room at the back, have you? We keep ourselves very much to ourselves here. You won't use the phone after eleven, will you?"

Anthony asked where the phone was.

"On the first landing. My flat is on the second landing. I have a *flat*, you see, not a room."

Light dawned. "Are you by any chance the other Johnson?"

The man gave a severe, almost reproving, laugh. "I think you must mean *you* are the other Johnson. I have been here for twenty years."

Anthony could think of no answer to make to that one. He went into Room 2 and closed the door behind him. On this mild, still summery day the room with its pipe-hung brick ramparts was already growing dark at six. He switched on the jellyfish lamp and saw how the light radiated the whole of that small courtyard. Leaning out of the window, he looked upwards. In the towering expanse of brick above him there was only one other window, and that on the top floor. The frilly net curtains behind its panes twitched. Someone had looked down at him and at the light, but Anthony's knowledge of the geography of the house was as yet insufficient to tell him who that someone might be.

Every morning for the rest of that week, Arthur listened carefully for Anthony Johnson to go off to work. But Jonathan Dean and the Kotowskys always made so much noise over their own departures that it was difficult to tell. Certain it was, though, that Anthony Johnson remained at home in the evenings. Peering downwards out of his bedroom window, Arthur saw the light in Room 2 come on each evening at about six, and could tell by the pattern of two yellow rectangles divided by a dark bar, which the light made on the concrete, that Anthony Johnson didn't draw his curtains. It was a little early for him to feel an urge to visit the cellar again, and yet he was already growing restless. He thought this restlessness had something to do with frustration, with knowing that he couldn't go down there however much he might want to.

On the Friday morning, while fetching in the post, he saw An-

thony Johnson come out of Room 2 and go into the bathroom,
wearing nothing but a pair of jeans. Didn't the man *go* to work?
Was he going to stop in there all day and all night?

Among that particular batch of letters was the first one to
come for Anthony Johnson. Arthur knew it was for him as it was
postmarked York and written on the flap was the sender's name
and address: Mrs. R. L. Johnson, 22 West Highamgate, York. But
the front of the envelope was addressed, quite ambiguously, to
A. Johnson Esq., 2/142 Trinity Road, London W15 6HD. Arthur
sucked in his lips with an expression of exasperation. And when,
a minute or so later, Anthony Johnson re-emerged, smelling of
toothpaste, Arthur pointed out to him the possible consequences
of such impreciseness.

The young man took it very casually. "It's from my mother. I'll
tell her to put Room 2, if I think of it."

"I hope you will think of it, Mr. Johnson. This sort of thing
could lead to a great deal of awkwardness and embarrassment."

Anthony Johnson smiled, showing beautiful teeth. He radiated
health and vigour and a kind of modest virility to an extent that
made Arthur uncomfortable. Besides, he didn't want to look at
bare brown chests at ten past nine in the morning, thank you
very much.

"A great deal of awkwardness," he repeated.

"Oh, I don't think so. Let's not meet trouble half-way. I
don't suppose I'll get many letters, and the ones I do get will either be postmarked York or Bristol."

"Very well. I thought I should mention it and I have. Now
you can't blame me if there is a Mix Up."

"I shan't blame you."

Arthur said no more. The man's manner floored him. It was so
casual, so calm, so poised. He could have coped with defen-
siveness or a proper apology. This cool acceptance—no, it wasn't
really cool, but warm and pleasant—of his reproach was like
nothing he had ever come across. It was almost as if Anthony
Johnson were the older, wiser man, who could afford to treat
such small local difficulties with indulgence.

Arthur was more than a little irritated by it. It would have
served Anthony Johnson right if, when Arthur took the post in
on the following Tuesday, he had torn open the letter from Bris-

tol without a second thought. Of course he didn't do so, although the postmark was so faint as to be almost illegible and there was no sender's name on the flap. But this one, too, was addressed to A. Johnson Esq., 2/142 Trinity Road, London W15 6HD. The envelope was made of thick mauve-grey paper with a rough, expensive-looking surface.

Arthur set it on the table on the extreme right-hand side, the position he had allotted to Anthony Johnson's correspondence, and then he went into the front garden to tidy up the mess inside, on top of, and around the dustbin. The dustmen had now been on strike for two weeks. In the close, sunless air the rubbish smelt sour and fetid. When he went back into the house the mauve-grey envelope had gone.

He didn't speculate about its contents or the identity of its sender. His concern with Anthony Johnson was simply to get some idea of the man's movements. But on the following evening, the last Wednesday of the month, he was to learn simultaneously partial answers to all these questions.

It was eight o'clock and dusk. Arthur had long finished his evening meal, washed the dishes, and was about to settle in front of his television. But he remembered leaving his bedroom window open. Auntie Gracie had always been most eloquent on the subject of night air and its evil effects. As he was pulling down the sash, taking care not to catch up the fragile border of the net curtain, he saw the light, shed on the court below, go out. Quickly he went to his front door, opened it and listened. But instead of leaving the house, Anthony Johnson was coming upstairs.

Arthur heard quite clearly the sound of the phone dial being spun. A lot of digits, not just the seven for London. And presently a lot of coins inserted . . .

Anthony Johnson's voice: "I'm taking it that the coast is clear, he's not listening on the extension and he won't come up here and shoot me in the morning." A pause. Then, "Of course I'm teasing you, my love. The whole business is sick." Arthur listened intently. "I had your letter. Darling, I need footnotes. You must be the only married lady who's ever quoted *The Pilgrim's Progress* in a letter to her lover. It was *Grace Abounding?* Then I do need footnotes." A long, long pause. Anthony Johnson cursed, obviously because he had to put more money in.

"Shall I transfer the charges? No, of course I won't. Roger would see it on the bill and so on and so on." Silence. Laughter. Another silence. Then: "Term starts a week today, but I'll only be going to a few lectures that touch on my subject. I'm here most of the time, working and—well, thinking, I suppose. Go out in the evenings? Lovey, where would I go and who would I go with?"

Arthur closed his door, doing this in the totally silent way he had cultivated by long practice.

5

The air of West Kenbourne, never sweet, stank of rubbish. Sacks and bags and crates of rubbish made a wall along the pavement edge between the Waterlily and Kemal's Kebab House. Factory refuse and kitchen waste, leaking from broken cardboard boxes, cluttered Oriel Mews, and in Trinity Road the household garbage simmered, reeking, in the sultry sunlight.

"And we've only got one little dustbin," Arthur said peevishly to Stanley Caspian.

"Wouldn't make any difference if we'd got ten, they'd be full up now. Can't you put your muck in one of those black bags the council sent round?"

Arthur changed his tack. "It's the principle of the thing. If these men insist on striking, other arrangements should be made. I pay my rates, I've got a right to have my waste disposed of. I shall write to the local authority. They might take notice of a strongly worded letter from a ratepayer."

"Pigs might fly if they'd got wings and then we shouldn't have any more pork." Stanley roared with laughter. "Which reminds me, I'm starving. Put the kettle on, me old Arthur." He opened a bag of peanuts and another of hamburger-flavoured potato crisps. "How's the new chap settling in?"

"Don't ask me," said Arthur. "You know I keep myself to myself."

He made Stanley's coffee, asked for his envelope, and went back upstairs. The idea of discussing Anthony Johnson was distasteful to him, and this was partly because any conversation in the hall might easily be overheard in Room 2. Stanley Caspian, of course, would be indifferent to that. Arthur wished he too could be indifferent, but there had crept upon him in the past few days a feeling that he must ingratiate himself with Anthony Johnson, not on any account offend him or win his displeasure. He now rather regretted his sharp words about the imprecise addressing of letters. Vague notions of having to become *friendly*—the very word distressed him—with Anthony Johnson were forming in his mind. For in this way he might perhaps persuade Anthony Johnson to draw his curtains when his light was on, or provide himself with a venetian blind as an ostensible heat-retaining measure (Stanley Caspian would never provide one) or even succeed—and this would take much subtle and weary work—in convincing him that he, Arthur, had some legitimate occupation in the cellar, developing photographs, for instance, or doing carpentry.

But as he gathered up his laundry and stuffed it into the orange plastic carrier, he felt a fretful dismay. He didn't want to get involved with the man, he didn't want to get involved with anyone. How upsetting it was to have to *know* people, and how unnecessary it had been for twenty years!

~~~~~~~~~~

The psychopath is asocial—more than that, he is in positive conflict with society. Atavistic desires and a craving for excitement drive him. Self-centred, impulsive, he disregards society's taboos. . . . Anthony had been making notes all the morning, but now as he heard Stanley Caspian leave the house, he laid down his pen. Was there any point in beginning on his thesis before he had attended that particular lecture on criminology? On the other hand, there was so little else to do. The music from upstairs, which had been hindering his concentration for the past half-hour, now ceased and two doors slammed. So far he had met none of the other tenants but Arthur Johnson and, as fresh sound broke out, he went into the hall.

Two men were sitting on the stairs, presumably so that one of them, smallish with wild black hair, could do up his shoelaces. The other was chanting:

> "Then trust me, there's nothing like drinking,
> So pleasant on this side the grave.

It keeps the unhappy from thinking,
And makes e'en the valiant more brave!"

Anthony said hallo.

His shoelaces tied, the small dark man came down the stairs, extended his hand and said in a facetious way, "Mr. Johnson, I presume?"

"That's right. Anthony. The 'other' Johnson."

This remark provoked laughter out of all proportion to its wit. "Put that on your doorbell, why don't you? Brian Kotowsky at your service, and this is Jonathan Dean, the best pal a man ever had."

Another hand, large, red and hairy, was thrust out. "We are about to give our right arms some exercise in a hostelry known to its habituates as the Lily, and were you to . . ."

"He means, come and have a drink."

Anthony grinned and accepted, although he was already wondering if he would regret this encounter. Jonathan Dean slammed the front door behind them and remarked that this would shake old Caspian's ceilings up a bit. They crossed Trinity Road and entered Oriel Mews, a cobbled passage whose cottages had all been converted into small factories and warehouses. The cobbles were coated with a smelly patina of potato peelings and coffee grounds, spilt from piled rubbish bags.

Anthony wrinkled his nose. "Have you lived here long?"

"For ever and a day, but I'm soon to depart."

"Leaving me alone with that she-devil," said Brian. "Without your moderating influence she'll kill me, she'll tear me to pieces."

"Very right and proper. All the best marriages are like that. Not beds of roses but fields of battle. Look at Tolstoy, look at Lawrence."

They were still looking at, and hotly discussing, Tolstoy and Lawrence, when they entered the Waterlily. It was crowded, smoky, and hot. Anthony bought the first round, the wisest measure if one wants to make an early escape. His tentative question had been intended as a preamble to another and now, in the first brief pause, he asked it.

"What is there to do in this place?"

"Drink," said Jonathan simply.

"I don't mean in here. I mean Kenbourne Vale."

"Drink, dispute, make love."

"There's the Taj Mahal," said Brian. "It used to be called the Odeon but now it only shows Indian films. Or there's Radclyffe Park. They have concerts in Radclyffe Hall."

"Christ," said Jonathan. "Better make up your mind to it, Tony, there's nothing to do but drink. This place, the Dalmatian, the Hospital Arms, the Grand Duke. What more do you want?"

But before Anthony could answer him, a woman had flung into the pub and was leaning over them, her fingers, whose nails were very dirty, pressed on the table top. She addressed Brian.

"What the hell are you doing, coming here without me?"

"You were asleep," said Brian. "You were dead to the world."

"In the rank sweat," remarked Jonathan, "of an enseamed bed."

"Shut up and don't be so disgusting." She levelled at him a look of scorn, such as women often reserve for those friends of their husbands who may be thought to exercise a corrupting influence. For that Brian was her husband Anthony was sure even before he waved a feeble hand and said, "My wife, Vesta."

She sat down. "Your wife, Vesta, wants a drink. G. and T., a big one." She took a cigarette from her own packet and Dean one from his, but instead of holding out his lighter to her, he lit his own cigarette and put the lighter away. Turning her back on him, she struck a match and inhaled noisily. Anthony regarded her with interest. She seemed to be in her mid-thirties and she looked as if she had come out without attempting to remove the "rank sweat" of Jonathan Dean's too graphic description. Her naturally dark hair was hennaed, and strands of the Medusa locks—it was as wild and unkempt as her husband's but much longer—had a vermilion metallic glint. A greasy-skinned, rather battered-looking face. Thin lips. Large, red-brown, angry eyes. A smell of patchouli oil. Her dress was long and of dark dirty Indian cotton, hung with beads and chains and partly obscured by a fringed red shawl. When Brian brought her gin she clasped both hands round the glass and stared intensely into the liquid like a clairvoyant looking into a crystal.

Three more beers had also arrived. Jonathan, having directed several more insulting but this time ineffectual remarks at Vesta

—remarks which seemed to gratify rather than annoy her husband—began to talk of Li-li Chan. What a "dish" she was. How he could understand those Empire builders who had deserted their pallid, dehydrated wives for oriental mistresses. Like little flowers they were. He hoped Anthony appreciated his luck in sharing a bathroom with Li-li. And so on. Anthony decided he had had enough of it for the time being. Years of living in hall and rooming houses and hostels had taught him the folly of making friends for the sake of making friends. Sooner or later the one or two you really want for your friends will turn up, and then you have the problem of ridding yourself of these stopgaps.

So when Brian began making plans for the evening, a mammoth pub crawl, he declined firmly. To his surprise, Jonathan also declined, he had some mysterious engagement, and Vesta too, suddenly becoming less zombie-like, said she was going out. Brian needn't start asking why or who with and all that. She was free, wasn't she? She hadn't got married to be harassed all the time and in public.

Anthony felt a little sorry for Brian, whose spaniel face easily became forlorn. "Some other time," he said, and he meant it.

The sun was shining and the whole afternoon lay ahead of him. Radclyffe Park, he thought, and when the K.12 bus came along he got on it. The park was large and hardly any of it was formally laid out. In a green space where the grass was dappled with the shadows of plane leaves, he sat down and reread Helen's letter.

Darling Tony, I knew I'd miss you but I didn't know how bad it would be. I feel like asking, whose idea was this? But I know we both came to it simultaneously and it's the only way. Besides, neither of us is the sort of person who can be happy in a clandestine thing, an intrigue. Being discreet seems pointless to you, doesn't it, a squalid bore, and as for me, I always hated lying to Roger. When you said—or was it I who said it?—that it must be all or nothing, I, you, we, were right.

But I can't be very good at lying because I know Roger has sensed my defection. He has always been causelessly jealous but he never actually did things about it. Now he's started phoning me at work two or three times a day and last week he opened two letters that came for me. One of them was from mother and the other was an invitation to a dress show, but I couldn't get all upstage and affronted virtue with him. How could I? After all, I do have a lover, I have deceived him. . . .

A child, playing some distance off, gave his ball a massive kick so that it landed at Anthony's feet. He bowled it back. Funny, how people thought it was only women who wanted to marry and have children of their own.

I remember all the things you taught me, principles on which to conduct one's life. Applied Existentialism. I tell myself I am not responsible for any other adult person and that I am not in this world to live up to Roger's expectations. But I married him, Tony. Didn't I, in marrying him, go a long way towards promising to be responsible for his happiness? Didn't I more or less say that he had a right to expect much from me? And he has had so little, poor Roger. I never even pretended to love him. I haven't slept with him for six months. I only married him because he pressed me and pressed me and wouldn't take my no. . . .

Anthony frowned when he came to that bit. He hated her weakness, her vacillations. There were whole areas of her soft, sensitive personality he didn't begin to understand. But here was the Bunyan passage—that made sense.

So why don't I just tell him and walk out?—Leap off the ladder even blindfold into eternity, sink or swim, come heaven, come hell . . . Fear, I suppose, and compassion. But sense that was too short-lived. *It's because at the moment compassion is stronger than passion that I'm here and you're alone in London. . . .* He folded the letter and put it back in his pocket. He wasn't downcast, only rather lonely, more than rather bored. In the end she would come to him, her own feelings for him were too strong to be denied. There had been things between them she would remember in his absence, and that memory, that hope of renewal, would be stronger than any pity. In the meantime? He threw back the child's ball once more, rolled over on his side on the warm dry grass and slept.

The tube took Anthony one stop back to Kenbourne Lane. At the station entrance a boy of about ten came up to him and asked him for a penny for the guy.

"In *September?* A bit premature, aren't you?"

"Got to make an early start, mister," said the boy, "or someone else'll get my patch."

Anthony laughed and gave him tenpence. "I don't see any guy."

"That's what me and my friend are collecting for. To get one."

The children, those in the park, and the two at the station, gave him an idea. A job for the evenings and the occasional weekend afternoon, a job for which he was admirably and thoroughly trained . . . It was six o'clock. He let himself into Room 2, wrote his letter, addressed an envelope and affixed a stamp to it. The whole operation took no more than ten minutes, but by the time it was done the room was so dark that he had to put the jellyfish light on. Emerging, he encountered Arthur Johnson in the hall, and Arthur Johnson was also holding a letter in his hand. Anthony would have passed him with no more than a smile and a "good evening," but the "other" Johnson—or was that he?—turned, almost barring his passage, and fixed him with an intense, anxious, and almost hungry look.

"May I enquire if you are going out for the evening, Mr. Johnson, or merely to the post?"

"Just to the post," Anthony said, surprised.

The hopeful light in the other man's eyes seemed to die. And yet why should he care one way or the other? Perhaps, on the other hand, that was the answer he had wanted, for now he held out his hand, smiling with a kind of forced bonhomie, and said ingratiatingly:

"Then, since I am going there myself, let me have the pleasure of taking your letter."

"Thanks," Anthony said. "That's nice of you."

Arthur Johnson took the letter and, without another word, left the house, closing the front door silently and with painstaking care behind him.

6

The dustmen's strike had ended, Arthur read in his paper, on the last Monday of September. Two days later, on the first Wednesday of October, he heard the crashing of lids, the creak of machinery, and the (to his way of thinking) lunatic ripostes of the men, that told him Trinity Road was at last being cleared of refuse. He might have saved himself the trouble of writing to the local authority. Still, such complaints kept them on their toes; they had replied promptly enough. The brown envelope was marked: London Borough of Kenbourne and addressed to A. Johnson Esq., 2/142 Trinity Road, London W15 6HD. Arthur put it in his pocket. The rest of the post, a shoe shop advertising circular for Li-li Chan and a mauve-grey envelope, postmarked Bristol, for Anthony Johnson, he arranged in their appropriate positions on the hall table.

They were all out but for himself. From the phone call he had overheard, Arthur knew Anthony Johnson would be going off to college or whatever it was today, but he was relieved to have had assurance made doubly sure by the sight of the "other" Johnson, viewed from his living room window, departing at five past nine for the tube station. Not that it was of much practical assistance to him, as he too must go to work in ten minutes; it was simply comforting to know the man went out sometimes. It was a beginning.

He went back upstairs and slit the letter open with one of Auntie Gracie's silver fruit knives. *London Borough of Kenbourne, Department of Social Services.* Well, he'd have expected to hear from the sanitary inspector but you never could tell these days. *Dear Sir, in reply to your letter of the 28th inst., requesting information as to the availability of work in children's play centres within the Borough, we have to inform you that such centres would come under the auspices of the Inner London Education Authority and are not our . . .*

Arthur realised what had happened and he was appalled. That he—he out of the two of them—should be the one to open a letter in error! It would have mattered so much less if it had been someone else's letter, that giggly little Chinese piece, for instance, or that drunk, Dean. Obviously the letter must be returned. Arthur was so shaken by what he had done that he couldn't bring himself to write the necessary note of apology on the spot. Besides, it would make him late for work. It was nearly a quarter past nine. He put the envelope and its contents into his empty briefcase and set off.

The demolition men were at work and Auntie Gracie's living room—brown lincrusta, marble fireplace, pink linoleum—all exposed to the public view. There on the ochre-coloured wallpaper was the paler rectangle marking where the sideboard had stood, the sideboard into whose drawer he had shut the mouse. His first killing. Auntie Gracie had died in that room, and from it he had gone out to make death . . . Why think of all that now? He felt sick. He unlocked the gates and let himself into his office, wishing there was some way of insulating the place from the sounds of hammer blows and falling masonry, but by the time Barry lounged in at a quarter to ten, he was already composing the first draft of a note to Anthony Johnson.

Fortunately, there was very little correspondence for Grainger's that day, the books were in apple-pie order and well up to date. Arthur found the task before him exacting, and one draft after another went into the wastepaper basket. But by one o'clock the letter—handwritten, as typewritten notes were discourteous—was as perfect a specimen of its kind as he could achieve.

Dear Mr. Johnson, please accept my heartfelt apologies for having opened your letter in error. Considering the gravity of this intrusion into your private affairs, I think it only proper to give you a full explanation. I was myself expecting a letter from the council of the London Borough of Kenbourne in reply to one of my own requesting action to be taken with regard to the disgraceful situation concerning the cessation of a regular refuse collection. Reading the Borough's name on the envelope, I opened it without more ado only to find that the communication was intended for your good self. Needless to say, I did not read more than was strictly necessary to inform me that I was not the proper recipient. In hopes that you will be kind enough to overlook what was, in fact, a genuine mistake, I am, Yours sincerely, Arthur Johnson.

Who could tell what time Anthony Johnson would return? Arthur let himself into 142 at one-fifteen. The house was silent, empty, and the mauve-grey envelope was still on the hall table. Beside it, neatly aligned to it, Arthur placed the Kenbourne council letter and his own note, the two fastened together with a paper clip. When he returned from work just before five-thirty all the letters were still there and the house was still empty.

Alone in his flat, he began to speculate as to Anthony Johnson's reaction. Perhaps the whole incident would turn out to be a blessing in disguise. Anthony Johnson would read his note, be moved by its earnest rectitude, and come immediately upstairs to tell Arthur he quite understood and not to give it another thought. This would be his chance. He put the kettle on, set a tray with the best china, and left his front door on the latch so that Anthony Johnson would know he was expected and welcome. For, irksome as it was to entertain someone and make conversation, it was now of paramount importance. And how wonderful if, in the course of that conversation, Anthony Johnson should announce his intention of securing an evening job—as the letter had intimated he might.

He sat by the window, looking down. Li-li Chan was the first to get home. She arrived with a different young man in a green sports car, and ten minutes after they got into the house Arthur heard her on the phone.

"No, no, I tell you I very sorry." Li-li almost, but not quite, said "velly." "You give theatre ticket some other nice girl. I wash my hair, stay in all night. Oh, but you are so silly. I don't love you because I wash my hair? I say I do love you, I love lots, lots of people, so good-bye now!"

Arthur craned his neck to see her and her escort leap into the car and roar off in the direction of Kenbourne Lane. He waited. Vesta Kotowsky came in alone, looking sulky. There was one, Arthur thought, who could do with an evening at home to get that draggled, greasy hair washed. At five past six Anthony Johnson emerged from under the arched entrance to Oriel Mews. And as Arthur watched him approach, the tall well-proportioned figure, the firm-featured, handsome face, the mane of hair crowning a shapely head, he felt a stirring of something that was part envy, part resentment. Yet this wasn't evoked by the "other" Johnson's good looks—hadn't he, Arthur, had just as great a share of those himself?—or by his occupancy of Room 2. Rather it was that there, in the process of its mysterious unfair workings, fate had been kinder. Fate hadn't saddled this man with a propensity that placed his life and liberty at constant risk. . . .

The front door of the house closed with a thud midway between Arthur's pernickety click and Jonathan Dean's ceiling-splitting crash. Ten minutes went by, a quarter of an hour, half an hour. Arthur was on tenterhooks. It was getting almost too late for tea. Time he started cooking his meal. The idea of anyone even tapping at the door, let alone coming in, while he was eating was unthinkable. Should he go down himself? Perhaps. Perhaps he should reinforce his note with a personal appearance and a personal apology.

A car door slammed. He rushed back to the window. It was the Kotowsky car, and Brian Kotowsky and Jonathan Dean got out of it. There followed a resounding crash of the front door. A long pause of silence and then a single set of footsteps mounted the stairs. Could it be at last . . . But, no. Dean's room door banged beneath him.

Very uneasy now, Arthur stood at the window. And again Brian Kotowsky appeared. Arthur caught his breath in sharply as he saw Anthony Johnson also emerge from the house. He looked reluctant, even irritable.

"All right," Arthur heard him say, "but it'll have to be a quick one. I've got work to do."

They crossed the road, bound for the Waterlily. Arthur crept down the first flight. A low murmur of voices could be heard from Jonathan Dean's room and then a soft, throaty laugh. He went on down. From over the banisters he saw that the hall table was bare but for the inevitable cheap offer vouchers. Li-li Chan's shoe shop circular and the two envelopes for Anthony Johnson had gone. Arthur stood by the table, nonplussed. Then some screws of paper lying in Stanley Caspian's wastepaper basket caught his eye. He picked them out. They were the note he had written with such care and anxiety to Anthony Johnson and the envelope in which the council's letter had been contained.

The Inner London Education Authority told Anthony that they couldn't possibly say over the phone whether they had a vacancy for him or not. Would he write in? He wrote and got a very belated reply full of delaying tactics which amounted to telling him that he had better apply again at Christmas. At least the Kenbourne authority had replied promptly. Anthony smiled ruefully to himself when he recalled the evening on which he had received their reply. It had been fraught with annoyance.

Firstly had come that letter from Helen, a letter which was more like an essay on Roger's miseries. *I sit reading escapist literature and every time I look up I find his eyes on me, staring accusingly, and every little innocent remark I make he takes me up on "What's that supposed to mean?" "What are you getting at?" so that I feel like some wretched shoplifter being interrogated by the great detective. I started to cry last night and—Oh, it was awful—he began to cry too. He knelt at my feet and begged me to love him. . . .* Anthony had been so exasperated by this letter which, in his delight at receiving it, he had stood reading out in the hall by the table, that it was some minutes before he had even noticed that there was another one for him. And when he did, when he opened and read that ridiculous note from Arthur Johnson, his impatience had reached such a pitch that he had screwed it up and tossed it into the wastepaper basket. It was at this point that Brian Kotowsky had arrived and, deserted by the best pal a man ever had, had pressed him to accompany him to the Waterlily. There Anthony had been obliged to listen to a dissertation on the horrors of matrimony, the undesirable independence having a job of her own gave to a wife, and what Brian would do after Jonathan's departure he honestly didn't know. Obliged to listen, but not for more than half an hour.

Returning alone to 142, Anthony considered going upstairs to reassure Arthur Johnson. The man obviously had an acute anxiety neurosis. A better-adjusted person would simply have scribbled *Sorry I opened your letter* and left it at that. The circumlocutions, the polysyllabic words were pathetic. They breathed a tense need for the preservation of an immaculate ego, they smelt of paranoia, fear of retribution, a desire to be thought well of by all men, even strangers. But men like that, he thought, cannot be reassured, their deep-seated belief in their own worthlessness is too great and too long-established at fifty for self-confidence ever to be implanted in them. Besides, Arthur Johnson liked to keep himself to himself, and would probably only be further perturbed by an invasion of his privacy. Much better wait until they happened to meet in the hall.

In the week which followed he didn't encounter Arthur Johnson but he was again accosted by the children at Kenbourne Lane station.

"Penny for the guy, mister?"

"Where are you going to have your bonfire?" asked Anthony. "In Radclyffe Park?" He handed over another tenpence.

"We asked. The park keeper won't let us, rotten old bastard. We could have it in our back yard if my dad lets us."

"Old Mother Winter," said the other boy, "got the cops last time your dad had a bonfire."

Anthony went off down Magdalen Hill. The kids and their parents called it Mag-da-lene, just as they called Balliol Street Bawlial. How stupid these pseudo-intellectuals were—Jonathan Dean was one of them—to sneer at mispronunciations. If the people who lived here hadn't the right to call their streets what they wanted, who had? His eye was caught by the piece of waste ground, enclosed by its rusty tennis court netting. The authorities wouldn't let him do official social work, but why shouldn't he do some privately and off his own bat? Why not, in fact, think about organising November 5 celebrations on that bit of ground? The idea was suddenly appealing. He gazed through the wire at the hillocky weed-grown wilderness. On one side of it was the cutting through which the tube ran down to London, on the other the mountains of brown brick, broken woodwork and yellow crumbled plaster which was all that remained now of the demolished houses. Backing on to the ground rose the grey-brown rears of Brasenose Avenue terraces, tall tenements hung with Piranesi-like iron stairways. A man seen building a bonfire there would soon attract all the juvenile society in the neighbourhood. And he could rope in the parents, mothers especially, to organise a supper. The great Kenbourne Vale Guy Fawkes Rave-up, he thought. Why, he might set a precedent and they'd start having one there every year.

It was six o'clock on a Friday evening, Friday, October 10. If he was going to do it he'd better start on the organisation tomorrow. Work tonight, though. Seated at the table in Room 2, its gateleg propped up with Arieti's *The Intrapsychic Self*, Anthony assembled and read his notes.

Not to be classified as schizophrenic, manic-depressive or paranoid. Condition cannot strictly be allied to any of these. Psychopath characteristically unable to form emotional relationships. If these are formed—fleetingly and sporadically—purpose is direct satisfaction of own desires. Guiltless and loveless. Psychopath has learned few socialised ways of coping with frustrations. Those he has learned (e.g. a preoccupation with "hard" pornography) may be themselves at best grotesque. For his actions . . .

With a sudden fizzle, the light bulb in the jellyfish shade went out.

Anthony cursed. For a few moments he sat there in the dark, wondering whether to appeal for help from Jonathan or the Kotowskys. But that would only involve him in another drinking session. The gentle closing of the front door a minute or two before had told him of Li-li's departure. He'd have to go out and buy another light bulb. Just as well Winter's didn't close till eight.

Making for the front door, he was aware of footsteps on the landing above him. Arthur Johnson. But as he hesitated, glancing up the stairs—now might be an opportunity for that belated reassurance—he saw the figure of which he had only caught a glimpse retreat. Anthony shrugged and went off in search of his light bulb.

7

Arthur was certain he had given mortal offence to Anthony Johnson and thus had wrecked his own hopes. Now there was nothing for it but to watch and wait. Sooner or later the "other" Johnson must go out in the evening. He went out by day on Saturdays and Sundays all right, but what was the use of that? It was darkness that Arthur needed, darkness to give the illusion that the side passage, the courtyard, the cellar, were the alley, the mews, the deserted shadowed space that met his desires. Darkness and the absence of noisy people, car doors slamming, interference . . .

He could remember quite precisely when this need had first come upon him. The need to use darkness. He was twelve. Auntie Gracie had had two friends to tea and they were sitting in the back round the fire, drinking from and eating off that very china he had set out in vain for Anthony Johnson. Talking about him. He would have liked, as he would often have liked, to retreat to his own bedroom. But this was never allowed except at bedtime when, as soon as he was in bed, Auntie Gracie would turn off the light at the switch just inside the door and forbid him on pain of punishment to turn it on again. The landing light was always left on, so Arthur wasn't afraid. He would have preferred, in fact longed for, enough light to read by or else total darkness.

Mrs. Goodwin and Mrs. Courthope, those were the friends' names. Arthur had to sit being good, being a credit to Auntie Gracie. They talked a lot about some unnamed boy he supposed must be himself from the mysterious veiled way they spoke and the heavy meaningful glances exchanged.

"Of course it puts a stigma on a child he can never shake off," Mrs. Goodwin said.

Instead of answering, Auntie Gracie said, "Go into the other room, Arthur, and get me another teaspoon out of the sideboard. One of the best ones, mind, with the initial on."

Arthur went. He didn't close the door after him but one of them closed it. The hall light was on so he didn't put on the front room light, and as a result he opened the wrong drawer by mistake. As he did so a mouse scuttered like a flash across the sideboard top and slithered into the open drawer. Arthur slammed it shut. He took an initialled spoon out of the other drawer and stood there, holding the spoon, his heart pounding. The mouse rushed around inside the drawer, running in desperate circles, striking its head and body against the wooden walls of its prison. It began to squeak. The cheep-cheep sounds were like those made by a baby bird, but they were sounds of pain and distress. Arthur felt a tremendous deep satisfaction that was almost happiness. It was dark and he was alone and he had enough power over something to make it die.

Strangely enough, the women didn't seem to have missed him, although he had been gone for quite five minutes. They stopped talking abruptly when he came in. After Mrs. Goodwin and Mrs. Courthope had gone, Auntie Gracie washed up and Arthur dried. She sent him to put the silver away which was just as well, because if she had gone she would have heard the mouse. It had stopped squeaking and was making vague brushing, scratching sounds, feeble and faint. Arthur didn't open the drawer. He listened to the sounds with pleasure. When he did at last open it on the following evening, the mouse was dead, and the drawer, which contained a few napkin rings and a spare cruet, spattered all over with its blood. Arthur had no interest in the corpse. He let Auntie Gracie find it a week or so later, which she did with many shrieks and shudders.

Darkness. He thought often in those days of the mouse afraid and trapped in the dark and of himself powerful in it. How he longed to be allowed out in the streets after dark! But even when he was at work and earning Auntie Gracie wanted him to come straight home. And he had to please her, he had to be worthy of her. Besides, defiance of her was too enormous an enterprise even to consider. So he went out in the evenings only when she went with him, and once a week they went together to the Odeon that was now Indian and called the Taj Mahal. Until one night when old Mr. Grainger, catching him in the yard as he was sweeping up at five-thirty, sent him over to the other side of Kenbourne to pick up an electric drill some workman had been careless enough to leave behind in a house where he was doing a rewiring job. He'd tell Miss Johnson on his way home, he told Arthur, and he was to cut along as fast as he could.

Arthur collected the drill. The darkness—it was midwinter—was even lovelier than he thought it would be. And how very dark it was then, how much darker than nowadays! The black-out. The pitch darkness of wartime. In the dark he brushed against people, some of whom carried muffled torches. And in a winding little lane, now destroyed and lost, replaced by a mammoth housing complex, he came up against a girl hurrying. What had made him touch her? Ah, if he knew that he would know the answer to many things. But he had touched her, putting out his hand, for he was already as tall as a man, to run one finger down the side of her warm neck. Her scream as she fled was more beautiful in his ears than the squeaking of the mouse. He stared after her, into the darkness after her, emotion surging within him like thick scented liquid boiling. He knew what he wanted to do, but thought intervened to stay him. He had read the newspapers, listened to the wireless, and he knew what happened to people who wanted what he wanted. No doubt, it was better not to go out after dark. Auntie Gracie knew best. It was almost as if she had known why, though that was nonsense, for she had never dreamed . . .

His own dreams had been troubling him this past fortnight, the consequence of frustration. Each evening at eleven, before going to bed, he had taken a last look out of his bedroom window to see the courtyard below aglow with light from Room 2. It seemed a personal affront and, in a way, a desecration of the place. Moreover, Anthony Johnson hadn't been near him, had avoided all contact with him. Arthur wouldn't have known he was in the house but for the arrival, and the subsequent removal from the hall table, of another of those Bristol letters, and of course that ever-burning light.

Then, on a Friday evening just before eight, it went out. Carrying his torch, Arthur let himself out of his flat and came softly down the top flight. He had heard the front door close, but that might have been Li-li Chan going out. Both she and Anthony Johnson closed it with the same degree of moderate care. And it must have been she, for as Arthur hesitated on the landing he saw Anthony Johnson appear in the hall below him. Arthur stepped back and immediately the front door closed. Through its red and green glass panels the shape of Anthony Johnson could be seen as a blur vanishing down the marble steps. No one, Arthur reasoned, went out at this hour if he didn't intend to stay out for some time. He descended the stairs and, delaying for a moment or two to let the occupant of Room 2 get clear, left the house, crossed the lawn, and entered the side passage.

There was no moon. The darkness wasn't total but faintly lit by the far-reaching radiance of street lamps and house lights, and the sky above, a narrow corridor of it, was a gloomy greyish-red; the darkness, in fact, of any slum backwater. And this passage resembled, with the colouring of Arthur's imagination, some alleyway, leading perhaps from a high road to a network of shabby streets. The muted roar of traffic was audible, but this only heightened his illusion. He crossed the little court, all the muscles of his body tense and tingling, and opened the cellar door.

It was three weeks since he had been here, and being here at last after so much dread and anguish brought him a more than usually voluptuous pleasure. Even more than usual, it was nearly as good as the real thing, as Maureen Cowan and Bridget O'Neill. So he walked slowly between the jumbled metal rubbish, the stacks of wood and newspapers, his torch making a quivering light which snaked ahead of him. And there, in the third room, she was waiting.

His reactions to her varied according to his mood and his tensions. Sometimes she was no more than the instrument of his therapy, a quick assuagement. But there were times, and this was one of them, when strain and memory had so oppressed him and anticipation been so urgent that the whole scene and she in it were altered and aggrandised by enormous fantasy. So it was now. This was no cellar in Trinity Road but the deserted, seldom-frequented yard between a warehouse, say, and a cemetery wall; she no life-size doll but a real woman waiting perhaps for her lover. The light of his torch fell on her. It lit her blank eyes, then, deflecting, allowed shadows to play like fear on her face. He stood still, but he could have sworn she moved. There was no sanctuary for her, no escape, nothing but the brick wall rising behind her to a cracked cobweb-hung sky. His torch became a street lamp, shining palely now from a corner. On an impulse he put it out. Absolute silence, absolute darkness. She was trying to get away from him. She must be, for as he felt his way towards the wall he couldn't find her.

He touched the damp brickwork, and a trickle of water fell between his fingers. He moved them along the wall, feeling for her, grunting now, making strong gruff exhalations. Then his hand touched her dress, moved up to her cold neck. But it felt warm to him and soft, like Bridget O'Neill's. Was it he or she who gave that choking stifled cry? This time he used his tie to strangle her, twisting it until his hands were sore.

~~~~~~~~~~

It took Arthur rather a long time to recover—about ten minutes, which was much longer than usual. But the deed had been more exciting and more satisfying than usual, so that was only to be expected. He restored her to her position against the wall, picked up the torch and made his way back to the cellar door. Cautiously he opened it. The window of Room 2 was still dark. Good. Excellent.

He stepped out into the yard, turned to close the door behind him. As he did so the whole court was suddenly flooded with light. And this light was as terrifying to him as the beam of a policeman's torch is to a burglar. He wanted to wheel round, but he forced himself to turn slowly, expecting to meet the eyes of Anthony Johnson.

At first he saw only the interior of Room 2, the pale green flecked walls, the gateleg table propped by and piled with books, the primrose washbasin and that light glowing inside the pink and green polythene shade which, for some reason, was swinging like a pendulum. Then Anthony Johnson appeared under the swinging lamp, crossing the room; now, at last, staring straight back at him. Arthur didn't wait. He hastened across the court, his head bent, a burning flush mounting across his head and neck. He scuttled through the passage, let himself into the house and went swiftly upstairs.

There, in his own flat, he sat down heavily. Vesta Kotowsky had come up in his absence and pushed her rent under his door, but he was so upset he let the envelope lie there on the doormat. His hands were trembling. Anthony Johnson had returned within less than half an hour of going out. It almost looked as if the whole exercise had been a plot to catch Arthur. But how could he know? He would know now or know something. Probably he was looking for some way of getting back at him for opening that letter. On the face of it, that letter hadn't seemed very private, not like the ones postmarked Bristol would be, but you never could tell. It might be that this college of his had some sort of rule about students not taking jobs—Arthur admitted to himself that he knew very little about these things—and that he would be expelled or sent down or whatever they called it for attempting to do so. After all, what else could explain Anthony Johnson's enraged rejection of his note, his deliberate shunning of him, his sneaking out like that followed by his purposeful illumination of the courtyard just as Arthur was emerging from the cellar?

The euphoria he felt after one of his killings totally ruined, Arthur passed a bad night. He sweated profusely so that he fancied the pink sheets smelt bad, and he stripped them off in a frenzy of disgust. Li-li had put her rent envelope under his door at some time in the small hours. By half-past nine he had assembled hers, the two envelopes of the Kotowskys—Vesta insisted on paying her half-share separately from that of her husband—and his own, and was seated downstairs waiting for Stanley Caspian. No more rent from Jonathan Dean, who would be leaving today, thank God, and none to collect (thank God again) from Anthony Johnson, who had paid two months in advance.

The hall was cold and damp. It was a foggy morning, an early harbinger of the winter to come. Stanley stumped in at ten past

ten, wearing a checked windcheater that looked as if it was
made from a car rug, and carrying a huge cellophane bag containing cheese puff cocktail snacks. Arthur began to feel queasy
because the cheese puffs, orangey-brown, fat, and curvy, reminded him of overfed maggots.

Stanley split the bag open before he had even sat down, and
some of the cheese larvae spilt out onto the desk.

"Put the kettle on, me old Arthur. Have a 'Wiggly-Woggly'?"

"No thank you," said Arthur quietly. He cleared his throat. "I
was down in the cellar last night." Forcing the carefully planned
lie out with all the casualness he could muster, he said, "Looking
for a screwdriver, as a matter of fact. The wires had come out of
one of my little electric plugs."

Stanley looked at him truculently. "You're always grumbling
these days, Arthur. First it was the dustbin, now it's the elec-
tricity. I suppose that's your way of saying I ought to have the
place rewired."

"Not at all. I was simply explaining how I happened to be in
the cellar. In case—well, in case anyone might think I was
snooping."

Stanley picked cheese puff crumbs off the bulge of his belly
whose ridges seemed as if they had been artfully designed to
catch everything their possessor spilt. "I couldn't care less if you
go down the cellar, me old Arthur. Have yourself a ball. Ask
some girls round. If you like spending your evenings in cellars,
that's your business. Right?"

Somehow, though he had intended wit, Stanley had got very
near the truth. Arthur blushed. He was almost trembling. It was
all he could do to control himself while Stanley filled in his rent
book, banging in the full stops until it looked as if he would break
his pen. Arthur put it back in its envelope himself and, muttering
his usual excuse about Saturday being a busy day, made for the
stairs. Half-way up them, he heard Anthony Johnson come out of
Room 2 and use to Stanley—in mockery? He must have been listening behind the door—his own words of a few moments before:

"I was down in your cellar last night."

8

Winter's being out of stock of all but forty-watt light bulbs, Anthony had been obliged to go as far as the open-till-midnight supermarket at the northern end of Kenbourne Lane. This unsettled him for work, and when he saw Arthur Johnson coming out of the cellar its possibilities intrigued him. He had penetrated no further than the first room, but that was enough.

Stanley Caspian burst into gales of laughter. "I suppose you were looking for a screw?"

Anthony shrugged. Bawdy talk from a man of Caspian's age and girth disgusted him. "You've got a lot of wood and cardboard and stuff down there," he said. "If you don't want it, can I have it? It's for a Guy Fawkes bonfire."

"Help yourself," said Stanley Caspian. "Everyone's got very interested in my cellar all of a sudden, I must say. You weren't planning to have this here bonfire on my premises, I hope?"

Anthony said no thanks, it wasn't suitable, which didn't seem the reply to gratify Caspian, and left him to his rents. He walked over to the station where the little boys were once more at their post, and with them this time a black child. The white children knew him by now. Instead of asking for money, they said hallo.

"Why don't we have a bonfire on that bit of waste ground?" But even as he spoke he checked himself. Wasn't that the insinuating approach a child molester would use? "If you like the idea," he said quickly, "we'll go and talk to your parents about it."

Leroy, the coloured boy, lived with his mother in a ground-floor flat in Brasenose Avenue. Linthea Carville turned out to be

a part-time social worker, which gave her an immediate affinity
with Anthony, though he would in any case have been drawn to
her. He couldn't help staring at her, this tall daughter of African
gods, with her pearly-bloomed dark face, and her black hair,
oiled and satiny, worn in a heavy knot on the crown of her head.
But he remembered his plan, explained it, and within ten minutes they had been joined by white neighbours, the chairman of
the Brasenose Tenants' Association, and by the mother of Leroy's
taller friend, Steve.

The chairman was enthusiastic about Anthony's idea. For
months his association had been campaigning for the council to
convert the waste ground into a children's playground. This
would be a feather in its cap. They could have a big party on
November 5 and maybe invite a council representative to be
present. Linthea said she would make hot dogs and enlist the
help of another friend, the mother of David, the third boy. And
when Anthony told them about the wood, Steve said his elder
brother had a box barrow which he could bring over to 142 on
the following Saturday.

Then they discussed the guy Steve's mother said she would
dress in a discarded suit of her husband's. Linthea made lots of
strong, delicious coffee, and it was nearly lunchtime before Anthony went back to Trinity Road. He had forgotten that this was
the day of Jonathan Dean's departure. The move, he now saw,
was well under way. Jonathan and Brian were carrying crates
down the stairs and packing them into Brian's rather inadequate
car. Vesta was nowhere to be seen.

"I'll give you a hand," Anthony said, and regretted the offer
when Brian slapped him on the back and remarked that after
Jonathan had deserted him he would know where to turn for a
pal.

Jonathan, like Anthony, possessed no furniture of his own but
he had hundreds of records and quite a few books, the heaviest
and most thumbed of which was the *Oxford Dictionary of Quotations*. While they worked and ate the fish and chips Brian had
been sent out to buy, the record player remained on, and the
laughter sequence from Strauss's *Elektra* roared out so mania-
cally that Anthony expected Arthur Johnson to appear at any
moment and complain. But he didn't appear even when Jon-

athan dropped a crate of groceries on the stairs and collapsed in fits of mirth at the sight of egg yolk and H.P. Sauce and extended-life milk dripping from the treads.

They had to make several journeys. Jonathan's new home was a much smaller room than the one he had occupied at 142, in a squalid, run-down house in the worst part of South Kenbourne. And this alternative to Trinity Road seemed to perplex Brian as much as it did Anthony. What had possessed Jonathan? he kept asking. Why not change his mind even at this late stage? Caspian would surely let him keep his old room if he asked.

"No, he wouldn't," said Jonathan. "He's let it to some Spade." And he added, like Cicero but less appositely, *"O tempora! O mores!"*

The record player was the last thing to be shifted. A container was needed in which to transport it, so Brian and Anthony went down to Anthony's room where Anthony said he had found a cardboard box in the wardrobe. The books impressed Brian and soon he had found out all about Anthony's thesis, taking up much the same attitude to it as he would have done had he learned Anthony was writing a thriller.

"There's a study for you," he said as they drove past the cemetery. "You could use that in your writing. Twenty-five years ago last month that's where the Kenbourne Killer strangled his first victim. Maureen Cowan, she was called."

"What, in the cemetery?"

"No, in the path that runs along the back of it. A lot of people use that path as a short cut from the Hospital Arms to Elm Green station. She was a tart, soliciting down there. Mind you, I was only a kid at the time, but I remember it all right."

"Kid?" said Jonathan. "You mean you're *kidding*. You were thirteen."

Brian looked hurt but he made no response. "They never caught the chap. He struck again"—he employed the journalese quite unconsciously as if it were standard usage—"five years later. That time it was a student nurse called Bridget Something. Irish girl. He strangled her on a bit of open ground between the hospital and the railway bridge. Now would he be a psychopath, Tony?"

"I suppose so. Was it the same man both times?"

"The cops thought so. But there were never any more murders
—not unsolved ones, I mean. Now why, Tony, would you say
that was?"

"Moved out of the district," said Anthony, who was getting
bored. "Or died," he added, for he had been less than a year old
when that first murder was committed.

"Could have been in prison for something else," said Brian.
"Could have been in a mental home. I've often wondered about
that and whether he'll ever come back and strike again." He
parked the car outside Jonathan's new home. "What a dump!
You could still change your mind, Jon old man. Move in with
Vesta and me for a bit. Have our couch."

"Christ," said Jonathan. "There's one born every minute." He
delivered this platitude as if it were a quotation, as perhaps, Anthony thought, it was.

They invited him to accompany them to the Grand Duke for
an evening's drinking, but Anthony refused. It was nearly five.
He went home and read J. G. Miller's doctoral dissertation:
"Eyeblink Conditioning of Primary and Neurotic Psychopaths,"
remembering at ten to put his clock and his watch back. It was
the end of British Summertime.

~~~~~~~~~~

Watching from his eyrie, his living-room window, Arthur saw
the new tenant of Room 3 arrive on Sunday afternoon. At first he
thought this must be some visitor, a disreputable friend perhaps
of Li-li's or Anthony Johnson's, for he couldn't recollect any previous tenant having arrived in such style. The man was as black
as the taxi from which he alighted, and not only black of skin
and hair. He wore a black leather coat which, even from that
distance, Arthur could see had cost a lot of money, and he
carried two huge black leather suitcases. To Arthur's horrified
eyes, he resembled some Haitian gangster-cum-political bigwig.
He had seen such characters on television and he wouldn't have
been surprised to learn that a couple of revolvers and a knife
were concealed under that flashy coat.

Staying here obviously, but as whose guest? Arthur put his
own front door on the latch and listened. The house door closed

quietly, footsteps crossed the hall, mounted the stairs. He peeped
out in time to see a sepia-coloured hand adorned with a plain
gold signet ring insert a key in the lock of Room 3. He was in-
censed. Once again Stanley Caspian hadn't bothered to tell him
he'd let a room. Once again he had been slighted. For two pins
he'd write a strongly-worded letter to Stanley, complaining of ill-
usage. But what would be the use? Stanley would only say
Arthur hadn't given him the chance to tell him, and it was vain
to grumble about the new man's colour with this Race Relations
Act restricting landlords the way it did.

On Tuesday Arthur learned his name. He took in the letters, a
whole heap of them this morning. One for Li-li from Taiwan,
sender Chan Ah Feng; two for Anthony Johnson, one postmarked York, the other, in a mauve-grey envelope, Bristol. *Her*
letters, Arthur had noted, always came on a Tuesday or a
Wednesday, and were still addressed to A. Johnson Esq., 2/142
Trinity Road. Mrs. R. L. Johnson, however, had learned sense
and put Room 2. All the other correspondence, five official-looking envelopes, was for Winston Mervyn Esq., 3/142 Trinity
Road. Winston! The cheek of it, some West Indian grand-
children of slaves christening their son after the greatest Englishman of the century! It seemed to Arthur an added effrontery that
this presumptuous black should receive letters so soon after his
arrival—five letters to fill up the table and make him look important.

But he didn't see the new tenant or hear a sound from him,
though nightly he listened for voodoo drums.

~~~~~~~~~

As Anthony had expected, the departure of Jonathan Dean
was the signal for Brian to put on the pressure. He was marked
to succeed Jonathan, and evening after evening there came a
knock on the door of Room 2 and a plaintive invitation to go
drinking in the Lily.

"I do have to work," Anthony said after the fourth time of asking. "Sorry, but that's the way it is."

Brian gave him his beaten spaniel look. "I suppose the fact is
you don't like me. I bore you. Go on, you may as well admit it. I

am a bore. I ought to know it by now, Vesta's told me often enough."

"Since you ask," said Anthony, "yes, it'd bore me going out and getting pissed every night. And I can't afford it." He relented a little. "Come in here for a while tomorrow night, if you like. I'll get some beer in."

Brightening, Brian said he was a pal, and turned up at seven sharp on the Friday with a bottle of vodka and one of French vermouth which made Anthony's six cans of beer look pathetic. He talked dolefully about his job—he sold antiques in a shop owned by Vesta's brother—about the horrors of living always in furnished rooms, Vesta's refusal to have children even if they got a house, her perpetual absences in the evenings—worse than ever this week—his drink problem, and did Anthony think he was an alcoholic?

Anthony let him talk, replying occasionally in monosyllables. He was thinking about Helen's latest letter. It was all very well to talk of absence making the heart grow fonder, but "out of sight, out of mind" might be just as true a truism. He hadn't expected her letters to concentrate quite so much on Roger's woes. Roger had scarcely been mentioned during that summer of snatched meetings, that clandestine fortnight of love when a shadowy husband had been away somewhere on a business trip. Now it was Roger, Roger, Roger. *I ask myself if it wouldn't be better for both of us to try and forget each other. We could, Tony. Even I, whom you have called hyper-romantic, know that people don't go on loving hopelessly for years. The Troilus and Cressida story may be beautiful but you and I know it isn't real. We should get over it. You'd marry someone who is free and trouble-free and I'd settle down with Roger. I just don't think I can face Roger's misery and violence, and not just for a while but for months, years. I'd know for years that I'd ruined his life. . . .* Stupid, Anthony thought. Illogical. He and she wouldn't go on loving hopelessly for years, but Roger would. Of all the irrational nonsense . . .

He said "Yes" and "I see" and "That's bad" for about the fiftieth time to Brian and then, because he couldn't take any more, he bundled him out with his two half-empty bottles under his arm. Having drunk no more than a pint of beer himself, he set to work and was still writing at two in the morning. The coarse, talking-with-his-mouth-full voice of Stanley Caspian woke him at ten, and he waited until he and Arthur Johnson had gone before going to the bathroom. It was lucky he happened to be in the hall when Linthea Carville, her son, and Steve and David arrived, for it was Arthur Johnson's bell they rang. Anthony saw them silhouetted behind the red and green glass and, making a mental note that sometime he must put his own name under his own bell, he went outside and took them round the back to the cellar. Linthea had brought a torch and two candles, and the boys had the box barrow. They didn't take the barrow down but carried the wood up in armfuls.

He was impressed by Linthea's strength. She had a perfect body, muscular, but curvy and lithe as well, and the jeans and sweater she wore did nothing to impede those graceful movements which he found himself watching with a slightly guilty pleasure.

"There's more wood here than I thought," he said hastily when he realised she was aware of his gaze. "We'll have to make a second journey," and he pushed the door as if to shut it.

"Don't forget my boy's still down there," said Linthea. "They all are. And they've got your torch."

The training they had in common had prevented them from falling into the adult trap of doing all the work themselves on the grounds that they could do it faster and more efficiently than the children. But once the barrow was filled, they had left the boys to explore the rest of the cellar. Linthea called out, "Leroy, where are you?" and there came back a muffled excited call of "Mum!" which held in it a note of thrill and mischief.

David and Steve were sitting on an upturned box, the torch between them, in the first room of the cellar. They giggled when they saw Linthea. Carrying a candle, she went on through the second room, walking rather fastidiously between the banks of rubbish. Anthony was just behind her and when, at the entrance to the last and final room, her candle making the one tiny puddle of light in all that gloom, she stopped and let out a shriek of pure terror, he caught her shoulders in his hands.

Her fear was momentary. The shriek died away into a cascade of West Indian merriment, and she ran forward, shaking off Anthony's hands, to catch hold of the boy who was hiding in a corner. Then and only then did he see what she had seen and which had sent that frightened thrill through her. As the candlelight danced, as the woman caught the laughing boy, the torch beam levelled from behind him by Steve, showed him the pale figure leaning against the wall, a black handbag hooked over one stiff arm.

"You wanted to give your poor mother a heart attack, I know you," Linthea was saying, and the boy: "You were scared, you were really scared."

"They were all in it," said Anthony. "I wonder how on earth that thing came to be down here."

He went up to the model, staring curiously at the battered face and the great rent in its neck. Then, hardly knowing why, he touched its cold smooth shoulders. Immediately his fingertips seemed again to remember the feel of Linthea's fine warm flesh, and he realised how hungry he had been to touch a woman. There was something obscene about the figure in front of him, that dead mockery of femaleness with its pallid hard carapace as cold as the shell of a reptile and its attenuated unreal limbs. He wanted to knock it down and leave it to lie on the sooty floor, but he restrained himself and turned quickly away. The others were waiting for him, candles and torch accounted for, at the head of the steps.

9

November was the deadline Anthony had given Helen for making up her mind. It was nearly November now and he was due to make his phone call to her on Wednesday, October 30. The letter he had received from her on the previous Tuesday had dwelt less on Roger's feelings and more on her own and his. In it she had written of her love for him and of their love-making so that, reading it, he had experienced that curious pit-of-the-stomach *frisson* that comes exclusively when nostalgia is evoked for a particular and well-remembered act of sex. With this in mind, he knew he would want to refer to it in their telephone conversation, would use it to reinforce his pressures on her, and he didn't want that conversation overheard by the Kotowskys, Li-li Chan, or the new tenant of whom he had once or twice caught a glimpse.

Why not ask Linthea Carville if he could make the call from her flat? This seemed to have a twofold advantage. He would have complete privacy and, at the same time, the very making of such a request, involving as it would an explanation of his situation with Helen, would reinforce the friendship that was growing between Linthea and himself.

But by Tuesday, October 29, that situation had changed again. He retrieved Helen's letter from under the huge pile of correspondence for Winston Mervyn which had fallen on top of it, and tore open the envelope only to be bitterly disappointed. *On Wednesday when you phone I know you will ask me if I've come to a decision. Tony, I haven't, I can't. We have had a terrible weekend, Roger and I. First of all he started questioning me*

*about my movements during that fortnight he was away in the
States in June. I'd told him before that I'd spent one weekend
with my sister and apparently he's now found out from my
brother-in-law that I was never there. He made a lot of threats
and raved and sulked but in the evening he became terribly pathetic, came into my room after I'd gone to bed and began pouring out all his miseries, how he'd longed for years to marry me,
served seven years like Jacob (of course he didn't, I'm not old
enough) and now he couldn't bear to be frozen out of my life.
This went on for hours, Tony. I know it's blackmail but most
people give in to blackmail, don't they?*

He was glad now he hadn't made that request to Linthea.
Hedging his bets? Maybe. But the West Indian girl had seemed
more attractive to him than ever when he had had lunch with
her and Leroy after they had collected the wood and when they
had met again at the Tenants' Association last Saturday afternoon. And if, as it would seem, he was going to lose Helen, be
dismissed in favour of that sharpshooting oaf . . . ? Was it so
base not to want to jeopardise his chances with Linthea—her
husband, at any rate, was nowhere in evidence—by making her
think herself a second choice, a substitute?

Rather bitterly he thought that he didn't now much care who
overheard his phone call, for there would be no reminiscing over
past love passages. One who wouldn't overhear it, anyway, was
Vesta Kotowsky who rushed past him in a floor-length black
hooded cloak as he was coming up the station steps. He went to
the kiosk and bought a box of matches with a pound note, thus
ensuring a supply of tenpence pieces for his phone call. He was
going to need them, all of them.

Her voice sounded nervous when she answered, but it was *her*
voice, not heard for a month, and its effect on him was tempo-
rarily to take away his anger. That voice was so soft, so sweet, so
civilised and gentle. He thought of the mouth from which it pro-
ceeded, heart-shaped with its full lower lip, and he let her talk,
thinking of her mouth.

Then he remembered how crucial this talk was and what he
must say. "I got your letter."

"Are you very angry?"

"Of course I'm angry, Helen. I'm fed up. I think I could take it even if you decided against me. It's probably true what you said in your other letter, that we'd forget each other in time. What I can't take is being strung along and . . ." He broke off. The Kotowskys' door opened and Brian came out. Brian started making signals to him, ridiculous mimes of raising an invisible glass to his lips. "Can't," Anthony snapped. "Some other night."

Helen whispered, "What did you say, Tony?"

"I was talking to someone else. This phone's in a very public place." He shouted, "Oh, God damn it!" as the pips sounded. He shovelled in more money. "Helen, couldn't you call me on this number? I'll give it to you, it's . . ."

She interrupted him with real fear in her voice. "No, please! I'll have to explain it when the bill comes."

He was silent. Then he said, "So you're still going to be there when the bill comes?"

"Tony, I don't *know*. I thought if you could come here at Christmas, stay in an hotel here, and we could see each other again and talk properly and I could make you understand how difficult . . ."

"Oh no!" he exploded. "Come for a week, I suppose, and see you for half an hour a day and maybe one evening if you can get out of jail? And at Easter perhaps? And in the summer? While you keep on vacillating and I keep on trying to understand. I won't be any married woman's lap dog, Helen."

The pips went. He put in more money. "That was the last of my change," he said.

"I do love you. You must know that."

"No, I don't know it. And stop crying, please, because this is important. Your next letter is going to be very important, maybe the most important letter you'll ever write. If you'll come to me we'll find a place to live and I'll look after you and you needn't be afraid of Roger because I'll be with you. Roger will divorce you when he sees it's no use and then we'll get married. But your next letter's your last chance. I'm fed up, I'm sick to death of being kicked around, and it'll soon be too late." Anger made him rash, that and the threat of the pips going again. "There are other women in the world, remember. And when I hear you tell me your husband's so important to you that you're afraid of him seeing phone bills three months hence, like someone in a bloody French farce, I wonder if it isn't too late already!"

A sob answered him but it was cut off by the shrilling peep-peep-peep. He dropped the receiver with a crash, not bothering to say good-bye. But in the silence he leant against the wall, breathing like someone who has run a race. In his hand was one last twopence piece. His breathing steadied, and on an impulse he dialled Linthea's number.

As soon as she heard who it was she asked him round for coffee. Anthony hesitated. His conversation with Helen had become a jumble in his mind and he couldn't remember whether he had given her this number or not. If he had and she phoned back . . . ? No, he wouldn't go to Linthea's, but would Linthea come to him? She would, once she had got the upstairs tenant to listen for Leroy.

~~~~~~~~~~

Arthur had overheard it all, or as much of phone conversations as a listener can hear. Because he hadn't heard the women's replies he wasn't sure whether or not Anthony Johnson was going out. Please let him go out, he found himself praying. Perhaps to that God whose portrait with a crown of thorns hung in All Souls' church hall where his Sunday school had been, though neither he nor Auntie Gracie had ever really believed in Him. Please let him go out.

But the light from Room 2 continued to illuminate the lichen-coated court. He heard the front door opened and closed and then he saw what he had never seen before, the shadows of two heads, one Anthony Johnson's, the other sleekly crowned with a pin-pierced chignon, cast on the lighted stone. Arthur turned away, his whole body shaking. He threw back the pink floral eiderdown and seized the pillows one after the other in his hands, strangling them, digging his fingers into their softness, tossing them and grasping them again so savagely that his nails ripped a seam. But this brought him no relief and, after an excess of useless violence, he lay face downwards on the bed, weeping hot tears.

~~~~~~~~~~~

Linthea wore a long black wool skirt embroidered with orange flowers. The upper part of her body was covered with a yellow poncho and she had small gold pins in her hair.

"I dressed up," she said, "because you're expecting other guests. A party?"

He was a little disappointed because she hadn't dressed up for him. "I'm not expecting anyone. What made you think so?"

She raised eyebrows that were perfect arcs, black crescents above white moons. "You wouldn't come to me. Oh, I *see*. You're so fond of this exquisite little room with all its antiques and its lovely view of an old-world cellar that you can't bear to leave it. Do you know, that lampshade looks exactly like a Portuguese Man o' War?"

He laughed. "I knew it was a jellyfish but I didn't know what kind. The fact is, I may be going to get a phone call."

"Ah."

"Not 'ah' at all." Anthony put the kettle on, set out cups. "I'll tell you about it sometime. But now you tell me about you."

"Nothing much to tell. I'm twenty-nine, born in Kingston. Jamaica, not the By-pass. I came here with my parents when I was eighteen. Trained as a social worker here in Kenbourne. Married a doctor." She looked down at her lap, retrieved a fallen gold pin. "He died of cancer three years ago."

"I'm very sorry."

"Yes." She took the cup of coffee Anthony gave her. "Now you," she said.

"Me? I'm the eternal student." As he said it, he remembered it was Helen who had dubbed him so, quoting apparently from some Chekhov play. She wasn't going to phone back. Not now. He began telling Linthea about his thesis, but took his notes gently from her when she started to read them. That sort of thing—*For his actions, cruelty to children and animals, even murder, he feels little, if any, guilt. His guilt is more likely to be felt over his failure to perform routine or compulsive actions which are, taken in the context of benefit to society, virtually meaningless*—no, that wasn't what he wanted to talk about tonight. Pity there wasn't a sofa in the room but just the tweed-patched fireside chair and the upright chairs and the thing he thought was called a pouffe. He sat on that because he could surreptitiously, and apparently artlessly, edge it closer and closer to her. He had got quite close, and quite close too, to unburdening himself about his whole disillusionment over the Helen affair, when there came a sharp rap on the door.

Phone for him. Come to think of it, he wouldn't be able to hear the phone bell in here. . . . He flung the door open. On the threshold stood the new occupant of Room 3, a tall, handsome man who looked rather like Muhammad Ali.

"I'm extremely sorry to disturb you," said Winston Mervyn in impeccable academic English quite different from Linthea's warm sun-filled West Indian. He held out a small cruet. "I wonder if you would be so kind as to lend me a little salt?"

"Sure," said Anthony. "Come in." No phone call. Of course he hadn't given her the number. He remembered quite clearly now.

Winston Mervyn came in. He walked straight up to Linthea who—if this is possible in a Negress—had turned pale. She half rose. She held out her hand and said:

"This is unbelievable. It's too much of a coincidence."

"It is not," said the visitor, "entirely a coincidence. The salt was a ploy. I saw you come to the door."

"Yes, but to be living here and in this house . . ." Linthea broke off. "We knew each other in Jamaica, Anthony. We haven't met for twelve years."

10

On the doormat lay three letters for Winston Mervyn, a bill for Brian Kotowsky, and the mauve-grey envelope from Bristol addressed to Anthony Johnson. Arthur, holding it in his hand, speculated briefly as to its contents. Had the woman decided to leave her husband or to stay with him? But he couldn't summon up much interest in it, for he was obsessed to the exclusion of all else by his need to secure absolute private possession of the cellar.

It had been frosty, the night preceding November 5, and a thick white rime stuck like snow to walls and railings and doorsteps. The yellow leaves which clogged the gutters were each edged with a tinsel rim. He put his hand to Grainger's gate and found that it was already unlocked. For once, Barry was in before him. Arthur saw him over by a load of timber, about to set a match to a jumping cracker.

"Stop that," Arthur said in a chilly, carrying voice. "D'you want to set the place on fire?"

He let himself into the office. Barry came and stood sulkily in the doorway.

"When I was your age I'd have been severely punished if I'd so much as touched a firework."

Barry blew an orange bubble gum bubble. "What's pissing you off this morning?"

"How dare you use such language!" Arthur thundered. "Get out of here. Go and make a cup of tea."

"What, at half nine?"

"Do as you're told. When I was your age I'd have thought myself lucky to have *got* a cup of tea in the morning."

When I was your age . . . Looking out of the window at the
white desolation, Arthur thought of that lost childhood of his.
Would he have been punished for touching a firework? Perhaps,
by the time he was Barry's age, he had already been deterred
from doing anything so obviously venal. Yes, he had been strictly
brought up, but he had no quarrel with the strict upbringing of
children.

"Until you are grown up, Arthur," Auntie Gracie used to say,
"I am the master of this house."

Laxity on her part might have led to his growing up weak,
slovenly, heedless about work and punctuality. And a greater
freedom would have been bad for him. Look what he did with
freedom when he had it—things which would, if unchecked,
deprive him of freedom altogether. Like the incident with Mrs.
Goodwin's baby . . . But before he could dwell on that one,
Barry had come in with the tea.

"You seen that bonfire they're going to have on the bit of
ground?"

"I like my tea in my cup, not in my saucer," said Arthur. "No,
I cannot say I have seen it. Who might 'they' be?"

"People, kids, I don't know. It's a bleeding great pile of wood
they got there. I reckon it'll be the best fire in Kenbourne. It's no
good you looking out of the window, it's right up against them
fences in Brasenose."

Arthur sipped his tea. "Let us hope there won't be any catas-
trophes. I imagine the fire brigade will have a busy night of it.
Now when you've finished helping yourself to Mr. Grainger's
sugar, perhaps you'll condescend to empty my wastepaper
basket."

A formidable pile of correspondence awaited him. He began
opening envelopes carefully. Once, hurrying, he had torn a
cheque for a large sum in half. But this morning a proper concentration was almost impossible to achieve. He knew, from the images which kept moving in procession across his mental eye,
from memories arising out of a past he had been used to think
eradicated, from the pressure and buzzing in his head, that he
was reaching the end of his tether.

Those images included, of course, dead faces; that of Auntie Gracie, those of the two girls. He saw the mouse, stiff, stretched, bloody. And now he saw the baby and heard again its screams.

Auntie Gracie had been minding that baby for its mother. There had been some sick relative, Arthur remembered, whom Mrs. Goodwin was obliged to visit.

"If I have to pop out to the shops," Auntie Gracie had said, "Arthur will be here"—and with a loaded look—"it will be good for Arthur to be placed in a position of trust."

Once she was out of the house, he had gone and stood over the baby, scrutinising it with curious desire. It was about six months old, fat, fast asleep. He withdrew the covers, lifted the woolly jacket it wore, and still it didn't wake. A napkin, white and fleecy, secured with a large safety pin, was now visible above its leggings. Safety was a strange word to apply to so obviously dangerous a weapon. Arthur removed the pin and, taut now with joy and power, thrust it up to its curled hilt into the baby's stomach. The baby woke with a shattering scream and a great bubble of scarlet blood welled out as he removed the pin. For a while he listened to its screams, watching it and exulting, watching its wide agonised mouth and the tears which washed down its red face. He watched and listened. Auntie Gracie was away at the shops quite a long time. Fortunately. He had to make things right to avoid her anger. Fortunately, too, the pin seemed to have struck no vital part. He changed the napkin which was now wet with urine as well as blood, washed it—how Auntie Gracie had congratulated him and approved of that!—and by the time she returned the baby was only crying piteously as babies do cry, apparently for no reason.

No harm ever came to the baby. It was, he supposed, a man in his mid-thirties by now. Nor had he or Auntie Gracie ever been blamed for the wound, if indeed that wound had ever been discovered. But he was glad for himself that he had known Auntie Gracie wouldn't be long away, for where else, into how many more vulnerable soft parts would he have stuck that pin had the baby been his for hours? No, she had been his guardian angel and his protectress, succeeded at her death by that other protectress, his patient white lady, garbed in her clothes. . . .

By one o'clock he hadn't replied to a single letter. Perhaps, when he had a good lunch inside him . . . He put on his over-coat of silver-grey tweed, a shade lighter than his steel-grey silk tie, which he tightened before leaving the office until it stood out like an arch of metal. On his way to the Vale Café, he paused for a moment to view the stacked wood. The pile stood some fifteen feet high and someone had flanked it with a pair of trestle tables. Arthur shook his head in vague, undefined disapproval. Then he walked briskly to the café, having an idea that the crisp air, inhaled rhythmically, would clear his pulsing head.

Returning, he was accosted by a young woman in a duffel coat who was collecting information for a poll. Arthur gave her his name and address, told her that he supported the Conservative Party, was unmarried; he refused to give his age but gave his oc-cupation as a quantity surveyor. She took it all down and he felt a little better.

Grainger's correspondence still awaited him and, thanks to his idleness of the morning, it looked as if he might have to stay late to get it all done. During the winter, when dusk had come by five, he liked to leave the office promptly at that hour. The streets were crowded then and he could get home, safe and ob-served, before dark. But he comforted himself with the thought that the streets would be crowded till all hours tonight. Already he could see flashes of gold and scarlet and white fire shooting into the pale and still sunlit sky.

But from a perverse wish to see the evening's festivities spoiled, he hoped for rain and went outside several times to study the thermometer. There had been a few clouds overhead at lunchtime. Since then the clouds had shrunk and shivered away as if chilled out of existence by the increasing cold, for the red column of liquid in the thermometer had fallen steadily from 37 to 36 to 35 until now, at five-thirty, it stood at 29 degrees.

The sun had scarcely gone when stars appeared in the blue sky, as hard and clear as a sheet of lapis. And the stars remained, bright and eternal, while those false meteors shot and burst into ephemeral galaxies. Arthur pulled down the blind so that he could no longer see them, though he could hear the voices and the laughter of those who were arriving for the bonfire and the feast.

At ten past six he completed his last letter and typed the address. Then, leaving his replies in the Out tray for Barry to post in the morning, he put on his overcoat, gave yet another tug to his tie, and left the office. He locked the gates. The Guy Fawkes celebrants were making what Arthur thought of as a most unseemly din. He came out into Magdalen Hill and approached the wire netting fence.

A small crowd of home-going commuters were already gathered there. Arthur meant to walk past, but curiosity mixed with distaste and some undefined hope of disaster, impelled him to join them.

The tables had been laid with paper cloths on which were arranged mountains of sandwiches, bread rolls, hot dogs, and bowls of soup. The steam from this soup hung on the air. There were, Arthur estimated, about a hundred people present, mostly children, but many women and perhaps half a dozen men. All were wrapped in windcheaters or thick coats with scarves. Already the grass was frosted and their boots made dark green prints on the frost. The lights in the houses behind shed a steady orange refulgence over the moving figures, the silvered grass, the ponderous mountain of wood, the whole Breughel-like scene.

One of the women brought to the stacked woodpile a box barrow filled with potatoes which she tipped out. These, Arthur supposed, were to be roasted in the embers of the fire. And very nasty they would taste, he thought, as he saw a man—a black man, they all looked the same to him—tip paraffin over wood and cardboard and paper and then splash it over the guy itself. The guy, he had to admit, was a masterpiece, if you cared for that sort of thing, a huge, lifelike figure dressed in a man's suit with a papier-mâché mask for a face and a big straw hat on its head. He was about to turn away, sated and half disgusted with the whole thing, when he saw something—or someone—that held him frozen and excited where he stood. For a man had come out of the crowd with a box of matches in his hand, a tall man with a blaze of blond hair hanging to the collar of his leather jacket, and the man was Anthony Johnson.

Arthur didn't question what he was doing there or how he had come to be involved in this childish display. He realised only that no man can be in two places at once. If Anthony Johnson was here—from the way the children cheered, an evident master of ceremonies—he couldn't also be at 142 Trinity Road. It looked as if he would be here for hours, and during those hours the cellar would be private and unobserved. It would be dark and very cold, solitudinous but, on this night of sporadic violent sound, sufficiently within the world to touch his fantasy with a greater than usual measure of reality.

A kind of joy that was both intense and languid filled his whole being. Until that moment he had hardly realised to the full how insistently urgent his need for the woman in the cellar was. None of his dreams, none of his frustration, had brought it home to him as the sight of Anthony Johnson, striking his first match, applying it to the timber, now did. But as he savoured his anticipation and felt it mount, he knew he must let it mount to its zenith. He had time, a lot of time. The culmination and the release would be all the greater for being sensuously deferred.

He stood there, trembling again but now with ecstasy. And he had no fear of the dark or its temptations. Happiness, contentment, was in watching Anthony Johnson apply match after match to that stack of wood until the flames began to leap, to crackle and to roar through the pyramid. As the fire became established, a sheet of it licking the feet of the guy, the first fireworks went off. A rocket rose in a scream of sparks, and along the fence, under the supervision of the black man, a child ignited the first in a long row of Catherine wheels. One after another they rotated in red and yellow flames. And those paler, stronger flames climbed across the guy's legs, shooting long tongues across the black suit in which it was clothed, until they leapt to its face and head, spitting through its eye sockets, catching the straw hat and roaring through its crown.

The hat toppled off. The suit burned and fell away. There was a grotesque indecency in the way white limbs, long and smooth and glossy, lashed from under the burning material until the fire caught them and began to consume them also. Arthur came closer to the wire. His hands gripped the rusty cold wire. The mask was now a glowing mass that flew suddenly from the face and rose like a firework itself before eddying in sparks to the ground. A child screamed and its mother pulled it clear.

The flames teased the naked face. It wasn't a man's face but a woman's, pale, blank, even beautiful in its utter dead calm expressionlessness. It seemed to move and come closer to Arthur until he could see nothing, no people, no cascading colour, no smoke, nothing but that familiar and beloved face. Then it was still and calm no longer. It arched back as if in parody of those burned at the stake. The great rent under its chin opened, gaped wide like a razor-made slash, and the fire took it, bursting with a hiss through the tear and roasting with a kind of lust the twisted face.

His white lady, his Auntie Gracie, his guardian angel . . .

11

The house at 142 Trinity Road was unlit, every street-overlooking window a glaze of blackness between dim drifts of curtain. The curtains on the top floor shimmered whitely like the lacy ball gowns of women who wait in vain to be asked to dance. Inside the house there was total, breathless silence. Arthur, leaning against the banisters, his hot forehead against cold smooth wood, thought he had never known it so silent—no tap of heels, no soft giggles, mutter of words, whistle of kettles, trickle of water, throb of heaters, thud of door, heartbeat of life. It was as if it had retreated into sleep, but the sleep of an animal which is awakened at once by the smallest sound or movement. He could awaken the house by going upstairs and setting in motion all the processes of a routine evening. He could switch lights on, fill his kettle, turn on the television, turn down his bed, close the bedroom window—and look down into that court, at last unlighted, but dispossessed for ever of its lure.

Rage seized him. He put on the hall light and took a few steps towards the door of Room 2. To destroy property was foreign to his nature, property was what he respected, but now if he could get into that room, he would, he thought, destroy Anthony Johnson's books. One after another he pulled open the drawers in Stanley Caspian's desk. Stanley had been known to leave duplicate keys lying about there, but they were empty now of everything except screwed-up pieces of paper and bits of string. Yet he must have revenge, for he had no doubt that Anthony Johnson had performed an act of revenge against him. All these weeks Anthony Johnson had been harbouring against him a grudge—hadn't everything in his behaviour shown it?—because he had opened that letter from the council. Now it was his turn, he who had done his best to make amends. Now some act must be performed of like magnitude. But what?

Turning away from the desk and the door of Room 2, his eye fell on the hall table. Something seemed to clutch at his chest, squeezing his ribs. All the letters were still there, undisturbed; the bill for Brian Kotowsky, the official-looking correspondence for Winston Mervyn, the mauve-grey envelope from Bristol for Anthony Johnson. No one had returned to the house since that morning, no one had removed a letter. Arthur put his hand over the Bristol envelope, covering it. A light, constant tremor animated his hand, a tremor that had been there, electrifying his hands and his body with a delicate, frenetic throb from the moment he had witnessed that fire and its consequences. Blood beat in his head as if it were feeding an engine.

He thought now of the telephone call he had overheard. "Your next letter's our last chance. . . ." Her next letter. It lay under his trembling hand. Arthur lifted it up, holding it by its edge as if its centre were red-hot. Words of Auntie Gracie's trickled across his brain.

"Other people's correspondence is sacrosanct, Arthur. To open someone else's letter is the action of a thief."

But she was gone from him, never more to guard him, never more to watch and save. . . . He ripped open the envelope, splitting it so savagely that it tore into two pieces. He pulled the letter out. It was typewritten, not on mauve-grey paper but on flimsy such as is used for duplicates, and the machine was an Adler Standard like the one in his office at Grainger's.

Darling Tony, I think I've changed a lot since I spoke to you. Perhaps I've grown up. Suddenly I realised when you put the phone down that you were right, I can't hover and play this insane double game any more. It came quite clearly to me that I have to choose directly between you and Roger. I would have called you back then and there, but I don't know your number— isn't that absurd? I only know your landlord's got a name like a river or a sea.

I have chosen, Tony. I've chosen you, absolutely and finally.

For ever? I hope so. But I promised for ever once before, so I'm
chary of making that vast dreadful promise again. But I will
leave Roger and I will marry you if you still want me.

Don't be angry, I haven't told Roger yet. I'm afraid, of course
I am, but it isn't only that. I can't tell him I'm leaving him with-
out having anywhere to go or anyone to go to. All you have to do
for me to tell him is to write—write to me at work—and let me
know where and when to meet you. If my letter gets to you by
Tuesday, you should be able to get yours to me by Friday at the
latest. Of course, what I really mean is I want word from you
that you aren't too disgusted with me to need me any more. I
will do whatever you say. Command me.

Tony, forgive me. I have played fast and loose with you like
"a right gypsy." But no longer. We could be together by Satur-
day. Say we will be and I will come even if I have to run from
Roger in my nightdress. I will be another Mary Stuart and fol-
low you to the ends of the earth in my shift. I love you. H.

Arthur felt a surge of power. Just as the control of his destiny,
his peace, had lain in Anthony Johnson's hands, so the other
man's now lay in his. An eye for an eye, a tooth for a tooth. Anthony Johnson had taken away his white lady; now he would
take from Anthony Johnson *his* woman, rob him as he had been
robbed of his last chance.

He screwed up the letter and envelope and thrust them into
his pocket. He walked down the hall and came to the foot of the
stairs. How terrible and beautiful the silence was! With something like anguish, he thought of the cellar, unguarded, un-
watched. Wasn't it possible he could still get some relief from it,
from its atmosphere that had fed his fantasy, from an imagination that could still perhaps provide, furnishing her absence with
vision and empty air with flesh? He turned off the light, left the
house and made his way down the side passage. But he had no
torch, only a box of matches in his pocket. One of these he lit as
he passed through the first and second rooms. He lit another and
in its flare saw the heap of clothes on the floor, Auntie Gracie's
dress, the bag, the shoes, and scattered all of them like so much
trash as if they had never clothed a passion.

It was the death of a fantasy. His imagination shrivelled, and he was just an embittered man in a dirty cellar looking at a pile of old clothes. The match burned down in his fingers; its flame caught the box which suddenly flared into a small brilliant fire. Arthur dropped it, stamped on it. He caught his breath on a sob in the darkness, stumbled back through the thick darkness, feeling his way to the steps.

Through the passage to the front he walked. He turned to the right, crossed the grass, set his foot on the bottom step. Like others before him, he would have been safe if he had not paused and looked back. The mouth of the dark opened and called him. The jaws of darkness received him, the streets received him, taking him into their arteries like a grain of poison.

~~~~~~~~~~

The tables were bare, the fire had burned out, and the only fireworks which remained were those sparklers which are safe for children to hold in their hands. Only they and the stars now glittered over the frosty, debris-scattered ground. Linthea had stacked her crockery into the barrow and now, having collected her son and Steve, left them with a wave and one of her radiant smiles.

Anthony and Winston Mervyn began dismantling the trestle tables which they would return to All Souls' hall. The last of the fire, a fading glow, dying into handfuls of dust, held enough heat to warm them as they worked. Winston, who seemed preoccupied, said something in a language Anthony recognised for what it was, though the words were unintelligible.

"What did you say?"

Winston laughed and translated. "Look at the stars, my star. Would I were the heavens that I might look at you with many eyes."

"Amazing bloke, you are. I suppose you'll turn out to be a professor of Greek."

"I thought of doing that," Winston said seriously, "but there's more money in figures than in Aristotle. I'm an accountant." Anthony raised his eyebrows but he didn't say what he wanted to, why was an accountant living at that grotty hole in Trinity

Road? "Easy does it," said Winston. "You take that end and I'll go ahead."

They carried the tables up Magdalen Hill and along Balliol Street. A Roman candle, ignited outside the Waterlily, illuminated in a green flash the cavelike interior of Oriel Mews. Anthony, walking behind Winston, realised that although he had been told what Winston had quoted, he hadn't been told why he chose to quote it. All Souls' caretaker took the tables from them, and Winston suggested a drink in the Waterlily. Anthony said all right but he'd like to go home first as he was expecting an important letter.

A hundred and forty-two was a blank, dark smudge in a street of lighted houses. Winston went in first. He picked up his letters from the table. There was nothing for Anthony. Well, Helen's letter didn't always come on a Tuesday. It would come tomorrow.

"That's more like it," said Winston. "I might get along and look at that tomorrow." He passed a printed sheet to Anthony, who saw it was an estate agent's specification of a house in North Kenbourne, the best part. The price was twenty thousand pounds.

"You're a mystery," he said.

"No, I'm not. Because I'm coloured you expect me to be uneducated, and because I live here you expect me to be poor."

Anthony opened his mouth to say this was neither true nor fair, but he knew it was, so he said, "I reckon I do. Sorry."

"I came to live here because my firm moved to London and now I'm looking for a house to buy."

"You're not married, are you?"

"Oh no, I'm not married," said Winston. "Let's go, shall we?"

Going out, they met Brian Kotowsky coming in.

"You look thirsty," said Brian. "Me, I'm always thirsty. How about going across the road and seeing if we can find an oasis?"

There was no way of getting rid of him. He trotted along beside them, talking peevishly of Jonathan Dean, whom, he said, he hadn't seen since the other man moved away. This was because Jonathan and Vesta disliked each other. Brian was positive Jonathan had phoned, but Vesta had always taken the calls and refused to tell him out of spite. They walked through the mews which smelt of gunpowder and entered the Waterlily just before nine o'clock.

In another public house, the Grand Duke, in a distant part of Kenbourne, Arthur sat alone at a table, drinking brandy. A small brandy with a splash of soda. When first he had set out on this nocturnal walk he had been terrified—of himself. But gradually that fear had been conquered by the interest of the streets, by the changes which had come to them, by the squalid glitter of them, by the lonely places at which alley mouths and mews arches and paths leading to little yards hinted like whispers in the dark. He hadn't forgotten, in twenty years, the geography of this place where he had been born. And how many of the warrens, the labyrinths of lanes twisting across lanes, still remained behind new, soaring façades! The air was smoky, acrid with the stench of fireworks, but now, at half-past nine, there were few people about. It excited Arthur to find himself, during that long walk, often the only pedestrian in some wide, empty space, lividly lighted, swept by car lights, yet sprawled over with shadows and bordered with caverns and passages penetrating the high frowning walls.

The pattern, twice before experienced, was repeating itself without his volition. On both those previous occasions he had walked aimlessly or with an unadmitted aim; on both he had entered a pub; on both ordered brandy because brandy was the one alcoholic drink he knew. Auntie Gracie had always kept some in the house for medicinal purposes. Sipping his brandy, feeling the unaccustomed warmth of it move in his body, he began to think of the next repetition in the pattern. . . .

12

There were strangers in the Waterlily, men with North Country accents wearing green and yellow striped football scarves. Brian Kotowsky struck up acquaintance with one of them, a fat, meaty-faced man called Potter, and that would have suited Anthony very well, enabling him to discuss houses and house-buying with Winston, but Brian kept calling him "Tony, old man" and trying hard to include him in the conversation with Potter. Before Helen's tuition, Anthony wouldn't have noticed the way greenish-ginger hairs grew out of Potter's ears and nostrils, nor perhaps been able to define Potter's smell, a mixture of onions, sweat, whisky, and menthol. But he would have known Potter was very drunk. Potter had one arm round Brian's shoulders and, having listened to the saga of Jonathan Dean's defection and Vesta's knack of losing her husband all his friends, he said:

"Rude to him, was she?" He had a flat West Riding accent. "And he were rude to her? Pickin' on her like? Ay, I get the picture."

"You've got one of her kind yourself, have you?"

"Not me, lad. I never made mistake of putting my head in the noose. But I've kept my eyes open. When a woman's rude to a man and he's rude to her, it means but one thing. He fancies her and she fancies him."

"You have to be joking," said Brian.

"Not me, lad. You mark my words, you haven't set eyes on him because him and your missus is out somewhere now being rude." And Potter gave a great drunken guffaw.

"I'm going," said Anthony. "I'm fed up with this place." He

got to his feet and glanced at Winston who replaced the specifications in their envelopes.

They turned into the mews and were very soon aware that Brian and Potter were following close behind them. It was a little after ten.

"This is going to be splendid," said Winston in his cool, precise way. "They'll be drinking and rioting next door to me half the night."

But as it happened, Potter was unable to make the stairs. He sat down on the bottom step and began to sing a bawdy agricultural ballad about giving some farmer's daughter the works of his threshing machine. Anthony had noticed that Li-li wasn't in and that all the upstairs lights were off. That meant Arthur Johnson must already be in bed. Sound asleep too, he hoped.

"You'd better get him out of here," he said to Brian. "He's your friend."

"Friend? I never saw him before in my life, Tony old man." Brian had brought a half-bottle of vodka back with him from the off-licence and this he raised to his lips, drinking it neat. "Where am I supposed to put him? Out in the street? He comes from Leeds."

"Then he can go back there. On the next train out of King's Cross."

Brian looked helplessly at Potter, who was humming now and conducting an imaginary orchestra. "He doesn't want to go back there. He's come down for tomorrow's match."

"What Goddamned match?" said Anthony, who rarely swore. "What the hell are you on about?" He knew nothing of football and cared less.

"Leeds versus Kenbourne Kingmakers." Brian waved his bottle at Anthony. "Want some Russian rotgut? O.K., be like that. I'd never have brought him here if I'd known he was that pissed. I suppose we couldn't put him in your . . . ?"

"No," said Anthony, but as he was about to add something rude and to the point, Potter staggered to his feet and waved his arms, swivelling his head about.

"He wants the lavatory," said Winston. He took Potter's arm and propelled him down the passage. Anthony unlocked the door of Room 2 and, without waiting to be asked, Brian followed him in and sat down on the bed. He was flushed and truculent.

"I didn't like what he was insinuating about Vesta."

"He doesn't know her," Anthony said. "What's the use of listening to stupid generalisations about behaviour? They're always wrong."

"You're a real pal, Tony, the best pal a man ever had."

The lavatory flush went, and Winston came in with Potter who looked pale and smelt even worse than in the pub. Potter sat down in the fireside chair and lay back with his mouth open. Outside a rocket going off made them all jump except Potter, who began to snore.

"Give him half an hour," said Winston, "then we'll get some black coffee into him. In my ambulance-driving days I saw a lot of them like that."

"You've crowded a lot into your life," said Anthony. "Greek, accountancy, a bit of medical training. You'll be telling me you're a lawyer next."

"Well, I did read for the bar but I was never called," said Winston, and, taking Ruch's *Psychology and Life* from the bedside table, he was soon immersed in it.

"I didn't like what he said about my wife," said Brian. The vodka bottle was half empty. He glared at Potter and gave one of his shoulders a savage shake. Potter sat up, groaned, and staggered off once more to the lavatory. "He shouldn't have said that about Jonathan. Jonathan's the best friend I ever had."

Winston looked at him severely over the top of his book. "Make some coffee," he snapped. "Get on with it. You need it as much as he does."

Brian obeyed, whimpering like a little dog. He put the kettle on while Anthony got out coffee and sugar. Feeling suddenly tired, Anthony sat on the floor because there wasn't anywhere else to sit, and closed his eyes. The last thing he noticed before he fell into a doze was that Brian was crying, the tears trickling down his sagging red cheeks.

~~~~~~~~~

Arthur went into the gents, where he tore the Bristol letter into small pieces and flushed them down the pan. There was a finality in this act which both pleased and frightened him. No going back now, no possibility of restoring the letter with another explanatory note. The deed was done and his revenge accomplished. Would the knowledge of that be sufficient to sustain him till he was home again? Could he get home in safety? As he emerged once more into the cocktail bar, the fear of himself began to return. But all the same, he bought another small brandy. He was deferring his departure from the Grand Duke until the last possible moment. It was twenty minutes to eleven. In his absence, someone had taken his seat and he was obliged to stand in a corner by the glass partition which divided this section from the saloon. The glass was frosted but with a flower pattern on it of clear glass. Glancing through a clear space, the shape of a petal, Arthur saw a familiar profile some three or four yards away.

Fortunately, it was the profile and not the full face of Jonathan Dean that he saw, for he was sure Dean hadn't seen him. He moved away quickly, elbowing through the crowd. Dean's mouth had been flapping like the clapper of a briskly rung handbell, so he was obviously talking to an unseen person. Very likely, unseen *people*. Brian Kotowsky and maybe Anthony Johnson and that black man as well. Birds of a feather flock together. He must get out.

It was only when he was out in the street that he questioned that compulsion of his. If he meant to go straight home, what did it matter who saw him or what witnesses there were to his absence from 142 Trinity Road? Or didn't he mean to go straight home, but to wander the streets circuitously, the pressure in his head mounting, until the last permutation of the pattern was achieved? Arthur shivered. There was a bus stop a few yards down the High Street from the Grand Duke, but he didn't want a bus which would take him no nearer Trinity Road than the Waterlily. A taxi, on the other hand, would deposit him at his door.

Taxis came down this way, he knew, returning to the West End after dropping a fare in North Kenbourne. But the minutes passed and none came. Ten to eleven. Soon the Grand Duke would close and disgorge its patrons onto the pavement. On the opposite side of the street Arthur could see the edge of the thickly treed mass of Radclyffe Park. Its main gate was closed, but the little iron kissing gate, the entry to a footpath which skirted the park, couldn't be closed. He saw a woman pass through this gate, her shadow, before she entered the dark path, streaming across the lighted pavement. His heart squeezed and he clenched his hands. Maureen Cowan, Bridget O'Neill . . .

At last a taxi appeared. He hailed it feverishly and asked the driver for Trinity Road.

"Where might Trinity Road be?"

Arthur told him.

"Sorry, mate. I'm going back to town and then I'm going to my bed. I've been at the wheel of this vehicle since nine this morning, and enough is enough."

"I shall note down your number," Arthur said shrilly. "You're obliged to take me. I shall report you to the proper authority."

"Screw you and the proper authority," said the driver, and moved off.

The last K.12 bus would pass at two minutes to eleven. Arthur decided he had no choice but to get on it, but at the Waterlily stop avoid Oriel Mews and walk home by the bright lighted way of Magdalen Hill. Yet it took all his self-control to remain at that bus stop and not set off on foot, to take the way the woman had taken or to follow the serpentine course of Radclyffe Lane which, passing at one point between acres of slum-cleared land, at another between terraces of squat houses and mean little shops, at last came to the hospital, the bridge, and the grey-grassed embankment of Isembard Kingdom Brunel's railway. But as the temptation to do this became intolerable, the K.12 appeared over the brow of the rise from the direction of Radclyffe College.

Arthur went inside and the bus began to move. But it slowed again and stopped for the flying figure of a woman in a long, black, hooded cloak who had rushed from the Grand Duke to catch it. There were no more seats inside and she went upstairs.

The bus moved along fast because there wasn't much traffic at that time of night. It passed the cemetery where Maureen Cowan had plied her trade and where Auntie Gracie lay in the family plot beside her father and mother. It detoured along a one-way street and returned briefly to the High Street before turning up

Kenbourne Lane. And still, all along the route, red and green and silver flashes pierced the cold dark curtain of sky, breaking at their zeniths into tumbling cascades of sparks.

They took the right-hand turn into Balliol Street, and Arthur—who seldom rode on buses but who, when he did, was always ready to get off them a hundred yards before his stop—began to edge out of his seat. The black hooded shape was already waiting on the platform. Like a monk or a great bird, he thought. She was the first to alight, as if nervously anxious to get home.

The Waterlily was closed. All the shops were closed, and as he looked along the length of Balliol Street, he saw the light in the window of Kemal's Kebab House go out. But lights there were in plenty, amber squares dotted haphazardly across house fronts, street lights like wintergreen drops, the high-rise tower a pharos with a hundred twinkling eyes. Scattered on the pavement were the blackened paper cases of used fireworks. But there were no people, no one but he and the cloaked woman who fluttered away across the mews entrance towards Camera Street. An occasional car passed.

Arthur stood still. He looked through the window of the public bar of the Waterlily, but he watched the woman from the corner of his eye. A cruising car had drawn up beside her, delaying her. The driver was saying something. Arthur thought he would count up to ten, by which time she would have turned into Camera Street or gone with the man, be lost to him, he and she safe, and then he would turn and make for Magdalen Hill. But before he had got to five, he saw her recoil sharply from the car and begin to run back the way she had come. His heart ticked, it swelled and pounded. There were three white posts under the mews arch. No car could pass into it from this end. But she passed into it. The car seemed to give a shrug before it slid away down the hill, leaving her for easier, more complaisant prey.

Arthur too went into Oriel Mews, walking softly as a cat. It was dark in there, sensuously, beautifully dark. She was walking fast—he could just make out the grotesque flapping shape of her —but he walked faster, passing her and hearing the sharp intake of her breath as he brushed the skirts of her cloak.

Then, behind him, she fell back, as he had known she would. She would linger until she saw his silhouette against the lighted mouth at the Trinity Road end, until she saw him disappear. He let her see him. But instead of stepping out into the light, he pressed himself against the cold bricks of the mews wall and eased back a yard, two yards. He smelt her. He couldn't see her.

His tie was very tightly fastened and he had to wrench at it to get it off. His strength was such that if it had indeed been made of the metal it resembled he would still have possessed the power to get it free. Fireworks were hissing and breaking in his head now. The last of them fell into a million stars as the flapping hooded creature closed upon him and he upon her.

She didn't cry out. The sound she made came to his acute ears only, the gurgle of ultimate terror, and the smell of her terror was for his nostrils alone. He never felt the touch of her hands. She fell on the stones like a great dying bird, and Arthur, rocking with an inner tumult, let her weight rest heavily on his shoes until at last, precisely and fastidiously, he shifted his feet away.

13

When Anthony opened his eyes it was twenty past eleven. Winston was still reading *Psychology and Life*, Potter was still asleep. Both bars of the electric fire were on and the room was very hot.

"Where's Brian?"

Winston closed the book. "He went off about half an hour ago. Said he was going to find this Dean character and have it out with him."

"Oh God," said Anthony. "Let's get rid of Potter."

"When you like," said Winston equably. "I looked through his pockets while you were asleep. He's got plenty of money and he's staying at the Fleur Hotel in Judd Street."

"Well done, Sergeant. You'll go far." A thought struck Anthony. "You were never in the police, were you?"

Winston grinned. "No, I never was. Shall we get him a cab?"

Anthony nodded and they managed to wake Potter. But, as always on waking, Potter had a call of nature or wanted to be sick. He departed for the lavatory, and Anthony and Winston waited for him in silence. They had to wait a long time, as it was fully ten minutes before Potter reappeared, green-faced, unsteady, and drooling.

~~~~~~~~~

Arthur came through the front door of 142 Trinity Road at twenty-five to twelve. He held his coat collar high up against his throat so that the absence of a tie wouldn't be noticed. The bitter cold made such an action natural in someone who might be thought bronchial. But there was no one to see him and he wasn't afraid.

At first the house appeared as dark as when he had left it all those hours before. No light showed in Li-li Chan's window or in that of Winston Mervyn. The hall was dark and silent, but, pausing at the foot of the stairs, he saw a line of light under the door of Room 2, and the ill-fitting lavatory door had a narrow rim of light all the way round its rectangle. Anthony Johnson. It could be no one else. Arthur moved soundlessly up the stairs, but before he reached the first landing, six steps before, he heard the lavatory door open and saw a blaze of light stream into the hall below. It seemed to him that Anthony Johnson must have paused, must be looking up the stairs—for why else should he hang about in the hall? He didn't look down and by the time he was on the landing, he heard the door of Room 2 close.

Light flooded the courtyard below his bedroom window. But it was of no importance. The only danger to him lay in his being actually caught in the act of a killing, for he had been a stranger to the woman he had strangled, as he had been a stranger to Maureen Cowan and Bridget O'Neill. No one would care what time Arthur Johnson had come home that night because no one would think it necessary to enquire.

There was nothing to worry about. These were perhaps the only moments in his life when he had nothing to worry about. He savoured them, excluding thought, feeling an exquisite peace, an animal's well-being. Not bothering, for once, to wash, he stripped off his clothes, leaving on top of the heap of them the stretched, twisted silver tie, and fell beneath the blue floral quilt. In seconds he was asleep.

~~~~~~~~~~

It was always, as Winston pointed out, next to impossible to secure a taxi in Trinity Road which wasn't a through road and whose inhabitants in general couldn't afford cabs.

"We could get him up to the rank by the station."

"No, we couldn't," said Anthony. It had been bad enough lugging the somnolent, smelly Potter from Room 2 out into the street. He must have weighed at least sixteen stone. Now he sat where they had placed him, on the low wall that divided the patch of grass from the street, his head resting against the stump of a lime tree. The heavy frost that made them shiver had no effect on Potter who began once more to snore.

"I'll go to the rank," said Winston, "if you'll stay here and see he doesn't fall off on to the grass." But as he spoke a taxi cruised out of Magdalen Hill and came to a stop outside 142. Li-li Chan, in a green satin boiler suit and pink feather boa, skipped out of it and thrust a pound note at the driver.

"Ninety-eight, lady," said the driver, giving her back two-pence.

"You keep change," said Li-li, waving it away. While the driver stared after her in gloomy disbelief, she uttered a "Hallo, it's fleezing," to Anthony and Winston and danced off up the steps.

"You wouldn't believe it," said the driver, "if you hadn't seen it with your own eyes." He scrutinised the coin as if he feared it might vanish in the wake of its bestower.

Winston grabbed Potter under one arm while Anthony took the other. They shoved him into the back of the cab. "This one's loaded and he's in no state to argue about your tip. Fleur Hotel, Judd Street. O.K.?"

"Long as he don't throw up," said the driver.

The night was growing quiet now and there had been no sound of fireworks for half an hour.

It took nearly an hour to air Room 2. Anthony was a long time getting to sleep and, as a result, he overslept. Waking at eight-thirty, he hadn't time to shave or wash much, for he was determined to get down to work in the college library by half-past nine. There was a stranger in the hall, a nondescript, middle-aged man who nodded and said good morning in what seemed a deliberate and calculating way. Anthony had made up his mind he must be a plainclothes policeman even before he saw the police car parked outside the house, and at once he wondered if this visit had any connection with Brian Kotowsky. Brian had gone out the previous night, intent on quarrelling with Jonathan Dean—intent perhaps on fighting Dean?

But none of the occupants of the car attempted to speak to him, so he crossed the road towards Oriel Mews. Here his pas-

sage was barred. The mews entrance was blocked off by a tar-
paulin sheet, erected on a frame some eight feet high, and none
of its interior was visible.

~~~~~~~~~~~

The sound of knocking had awakened Arthur just before his
alarm was due to go off. Someone was hammering on one of the
doors, Kotowskys' or Mervyn's, on the floor below. Then he
heard voices, Mervyn's and another's, but he was used to all sorts
of unnecessary wanton noise, made at uncivilised hours, so he
didn't take much notice. Ten minutes later, when all the noise
had stopped, he got up and had his bath. He cleaned bath and
basin carefully, mopped the floor, plumped up the blue pillows
and shook out the quilt, took a clean shirt and clean underwear
from the airing cupboard.

A tramping up and down the stairs had begun. Perhaps someone else was moving out. It would be just like Stanley Caspian
not to have told him. He went into the kitchen and plugged in
his kettle, wondering in a detached kind of way if the body of
the woman had yet been found. Imprudent of him really to have
done the deed so near home, but prudence, of course, hadn't entered into it. The evening newspaper would tell him, reveal to
him as to any other stranger, the known facts. And this time he
wouldn't collapse and be ill from the culminating traumas of it,
but would watch with relish the efforts of the police to find the
killer.

A good strong pot of tea, two eggs, two rashers of bacon, two
thin, piping-hot pieces of toast. If they had found the body, he
thought as he washed up, they would in some way cordon off the
mews. Its entrance was just visible from his living room window.
His curiosity irresistible, he peered out between the crossover
frilled net curtains. Yes, Oriel Mews was cordoned off, its arch
blanked out with a big opaque sheet of something. A van had
probably gone in to load or unload and the driver had found her.
He scanned the area for police cars, found nothing until, focus-
sing closer, he saw one where he least expected it, right under the
window at the kerb.

Arthur's heart gave a great lurch, and suddenly his chest

seemed full of scalding liquid. But they couldn't know, they couldn't have come for him. . . . No one had seen him go into the mews and there was nothing to connect him with the dead woman. Pull yourself together, he told himself in the admonishing Auntie Gracie voice he kept for moments like this. Not that there ever had been a moment like this before.

He had slumped into a chair and now, looking down at his hands, he saw that he was holding the dishcloth just as he had held that silver tie last night, taut, his fingers flexed at its ends. He relaxed them. Was it possible the police car was parked outside because earlier there had been no other space in which to park? Again he looked out of the window. Anthony Johnson was crossing the road towards the closed mews. The long trill of his doorbell ringing seemed to go through the soft tissues of Arthur's brain like a knife. He swayed. Then he went to the door.

"Mr. Johnson?"

Arthur nodded, his face shrivelling with pallor.

"I'd like a word with you. May I come in?"

The man didn't wait for permission. He stepped into the flat and showed Arthur his warrant card. Detective Inspector Glass. A tall, lean man was Inspector Glass with a broad, flat bill of a nose and a thin mouth that parted to show big yellow dentures.

"There's been a murder, Mr. Johnson. In view of that, I'd be glad if you'd tell me what your movements were last evening."

"My movements?" Arthur had rehearsed nothing. He was totally unprepared. "What do you mean?"

"It's quite simple. I'd just like to know how you spent last evening."

"I was here, in my flat. I was here from the time I got in from work at six-thirty. I didn't go out."

"Alone?"

Arthur nodded. He felt faint, sick. The man didn't believe him. A blank, almost disgusted, incredulity showed in his face, and his lip curled above those hideous teeth.

"According to my information, you spent the evening with Mr. Winston Mervyn, Mr. Brian Kotowsky and a man called Potter."

And now Arthur didn't understand at all. Fleeting images of

the Grand Duke, of Dean's profile, appeared on his mind's eye, but surely . . . Then came light.

"I think you are mistaking me for Mr. *Anthony* Johnson who lives on the ground floor. Room 2." Firmly now, as he saw he had been right, that Glass had made a mistake, he added, "I was at home on my own all evening."

"Sorry about that, Mr. Johnson. An understandable confusion. Then you can't help us as to the whereabouts of Mr. Kotowsky?"

"I know nothing about it. I hardly know him. I keep myself to myself." But Arthur had to know, had to discover before Glass departed, why he had come to this house—why here? "This murder—you're connecting Mr. Kotowsky with it?"

"Inevitably, Mr. Johnson," said Glass, opening the front door. "It is Mrs. Vesta Kotowsky who has been murdered."

14

Anthony spent the day in the college library and it was nearly five when he reached Kenbourne Lane tube station on his way home. There on the newsboards he read: *Murder of Kenbourne Woman* and *Kenbourne Killer slays again?* Though he was necessarily interested in what leads men to kill, murder itself fascinated him not at all, so he didn't buy a paper. Helen's letter would be waiting for him, and since leaving the library his whole mind had been possessed by speculating as to what she would say.

The hall table was piled with correspondence, a heap of it, for once not carefully arranged. Anthony leafed through it. Three specifications from estate agents for Winston, Li-li's Taiwan letter, a bill for Brian, a bill for Vesta, a bill that would have to be redirected for Jonathan Dean. Nothing for him. Helen hadn't written. For the first time since he had moved into 142 Trinity Road, a Tuesday and a Wednesday had gone by without a letter from her. But before he could begin to wonder about this omission, whether he had been too harsh with her, whether she was afraid to write, the front door opened and Winston Mervyn and Jonathan Dean—who as far as he knew didn't know each other, had never met—came into the hall together.

"When did they let you off the hook?" said Winston. "We must have missed you."

"Hook?" said Anthony.

"I mean we didn't see you at the police station."

Anthony thought he had never seen Jonathan Dean look so

grim, so spent, and at the same time so much like a real person without pose or role. "I'm not following any of this."

"He doesn't know," said Jonathan. "He doesn't know a thing. Vesta was murdered last night, Tony, strangled, and Brian's disappeared."

~~~~~~~~~~~

They went up to Winston's room because it was bigger and airier than Anthony's. Jonathan looked round his old domain with sick eyes, and finding no hackneyed line of verse or prose to fit the situation, stretched himself full-length on the old red sofa. A freezing fog, white in the dusk, pressed smokily against the window. Winston drew the sparingly cut curtains.

"The police came here at half-past seven this morning," he said. "They couldn't get an answer from Brian, so they came to me. They wanted to know when I'd last seen Brian and what sort of a mood he was in. I told them about last night. I had to."

"You told them about all those insinuations of Potter's, d'you mean?"

"I had to, Anthony. What would you have done? Said Brian was sober and calm and went off to bed in a happy frame of mind? They rooted Potter out, anyway. He must have missed his match. Presumably, after that, they thought they wouldn't bother with you. And Potter must have remembered, hangover or not, because they got me down to the station and asked me if Brian had been in a jealous rage. I had to say he'd gone off looking for Vesta and *him*." Winston waved his hand in the direction of the recumbent Dean.

"But it was rubbish," said Anthony. "It was Potter's drunken fantasy. There wasn't any foundation for it, we all know that."

"But there was," said Jonathan Dean.

"You mean, you and Vesta . . . ?"

"Oh God, of *course*. That's why I moved away. We couldn't do it here, could we? In the next room to the poor old bastard. Christ, I was with her yesterday. We spent the afternoon and most of the evening together and then we went off for a drink in the Grand Duke. She left me just before eleven to get the last bus."

Anthony shrugged. He felt cold, helpless. "You said Brian had disappeared?"

Jonathan ran his fingers through his untidy ginger hair. "I haven't been living in that bloody awful hole for the past week. It stinks and it's overrun with mice. My sister said I could stay in her place while she's away in Germany. She's got a flat in West Hampstead. I went back there last night from the Duke. I got there about midnight and Brian turned up around half-past. He was pissed out of his mind and he was making all sorts of threats and accusations, only he passed out and I put him to bed."

"But how did he know you'd be there?"

"God knows. I've gone there before when my sister's been away." Jonathan shivered. "The thing is, Vesta could have told him before he . . ."

"Then where is he now?"

Jonathan shook his head. "I left him there and went to work. The fuzz got hold of me at about midday and I told them everything, but when they got to my sister's Brian had gone. They're searching for him now. It's no good looking like that, Tony old man, he must have done it. Why else would he vanish?"

"He could have gone out and seen an evening paper and panicked. I don't believe him capable of murder."

"D'you think I do? D'you think I like thinking that way about my old pal? We were like—like two red roses on one stalk."

Perhaps it was the crass ineptitude of this quotation, or that fact that, in these circumstances, Jonathan had quoted anything at all, which made Winston round on him. "If he did do it, it's your fault. You shouldn't have messed about with his wife."

"You lousy black bastard!" Jonathan turned his face into the sofa arm and his body shook. "God, I could do with a drink."

Not at all put out by the offensive epithets, Winston said calmly, "I wonder how many thousand times the ears of these walls have heard those words?" He shook Jonathan vigorously. "Why I didn't leave you on the steps of the nick for the dustmen to pick up I'll never know. Get up, if you want that drink. But we're not showing our faces in the Waterlily till all this fuss has died down."

"They say," said Barry, "as that bird as was done in lived in your house. Is that a fact?"

"Yes," said Arthur.

"Only they don't give you no number in the paper, just Trinity." Barry spooned sugar from the basin into his mouth and crunched it. "Here," he said, and thrust the *Evening Standard* under Arthur's nose.

The body of a woman, Mrs. Vesta Kotowsky, 36, of Trinity Road, Kenbourne Vale, West London, was found in Oriel Mews, Kenbourne Vale, early this morning. She had been strangled. Police are treating the case as murder.

The print swam. Other words were superimposed on it. *The body of a woman, Maureen Cowan, 24, of Parsloe Street, Kenbourne Vale, West London, was last night found in a footpath adjacent to Kenbourne Vale Cemetery. Police are treating the case . . . The body of a woman, Bridget O'Neill, 20, student nurse . . .*

Strangers to him, utter strangers. He had never even looked into their faces. Had he ever looked into any woman's face but Auntie Gracie's and Beryl's?

Beryl was Mrs. Courthope's daughter. When he came home and found her there one evening, drinking tea with Auntie Gracie out of those china cups he now possessed and cherished, he had been jealous of her presence. Who was she to break in on their cloistered world? And she had been there again and again after that, sometimes with her mother, sometimes alone. It was better when her mother was there because then Auntie Gracie stayed in the room too instead of leaving Arthur and Beryl together. He had never known what to say when he was alone with Beryl, and now he couldn't remember whether he had so much as uttered a word. He couldn't remember whether Beryl was pretty or plain, talkative or silent, and he doubted whether he had known at the time. He was indifferent to her.

But she liked him, Auntie Gracie said.

"Beryl likes you very much, Arthur. Of course, that's not surprising. You're steady, you've got a good job, and though I shouldn't tell you so, you're a very nice-looking young man."

Beryl started coming with them to the Odeon. Auntie Gracie always arranged it so that Beryl sat between them. He dared to say he had liked things better before they knew Beryl and had been alone together.

"There's no reason why we should ever be apart, Arthur. This is a big house. I have always intended you to have the top floor to yourself one day."

He didn't know what she meant or why she was hoarding her clothes coupons or examining so closely the best of the linen she had kept packed away for so long or talking of furniture being so hard to get in this aftermath of wartime. He didn't like being left with Beryl and talked about among Auntie Gracie's particular friends as if Beryl were his particular friend.

The night it had happened was the night Auntie Gracie had such a bad headache she couldn't face the Odeon and the film about American soldiers in the Pacific. Arthur said that in that case he wouldn't go either.

"You must, Arthur. You can't let Beryl down. She's been looking forward to going out with you all the week. You don't realise how fond of you she is. I know you're fond of her too, only you're shy. You haven't been friendly with any other girls, I'm glad to say."

Friendly . . . Beryl came to the house in Magdalen Hill and they set off together in silence. But when they had to cross the road she took his arm and held on to it all the way to the cinema. Her body was warm and clinging. Suddenly she began to talk. Her talk was madness. He thought she was mad.

"I've never had a boy friend before, Arthur. Mother wouldn't let me go out with boys till you came along. I know I'm not very attractive, nothing special, but I could have had boy friends. Now I'm glad I waited. Mother's told me, you see."

He said hoarsely, "Told you what?"

"That you like me very much, only you're too shy to say so. I like shy boys. I've been hoping and hoping for weeks you'd ask me to go out with you alone and now you have."

"My aunt's ill. That's why she hasn't come, because she's ill."

"Oh, *Arthur.* You don't have to pretend any more. I know you've been trying to put her off coming with us for weeks and weeks."

They went into the cinema. Sweets were just coming back into the shops. He bought her a bag of things called Raspberry Ruffles and muttered to her that he had to go to the gents. "I want to be excused," was what he said like you said in school. There was an emergency exit between the foyer and the lavatory. Arthur walked straight out of it into the street. He walked and walked until he had put two miles between himself and Beryl, and then, for the first time in his life, he went into a pub. There he drank brandy because he didn't know what else to order.

Soon after ten he left and began to walk home along the path that bordered the cemetery. There was a girl standing near the end of the path, and as he came up to her she said good evening. Later, he had learned she was a prostitute, waiting for the pubs to turn out, though at the time he had scarcely known of the existence of prostitutes.

He went up to her and put his hand into his pocket where he had stuffed his scarf. Perhaps she thought he was feeling for his wallet, for she moved towards him and put her hand on his arm. He strangled her then, and she was too surprised to struggle or cry out. Afterwards, when he understood what he had done, he knew he would be caught, tried, hanged—but nothing had happened. The police never came to the house in Magadalen Hill, and if they had they would have discovered nothing, for Beryl told neither his aunt nor her mother that he had left her alone in the Odeon. She gave them the impression that it was she who had jilted him, left him finally at eleven that night and never wanted to see him again. Auntie Gracie was hot against her for her ingratitude and her fickleness, and of course she understood why Arthur, disappointed in love, fell ill suddenly from some virus the doctors couldn't diagnose and was off work for six weeks. He never saw Beryl again, though later he heard that she had married a greengrocer and had two children. . . .

"Reckon her old man done it," said Barry.

Arthur couldn't summon the energy necessary to rebuke Barry for this slangy, coarse, and ungrammatical usage. He digested the sense behind the words. They would suppose Kotowsky had done it. Glass, evidently, already supposed so. But Arthur was still unable to struggle out of the paralysis of fear in which he had been gripped since eight-thirty. Impossible to get over the fact—yet equally impossible to grasp the full significance of it—that he had not only killed a woman he knew but one who lived in the same house. Impossible too to forget or come to terms with another aspect. He had lied to Inspector Glass, that piranha-faced man, lied under the pressure of panic and forgetting that his lie could easily be detected. Anthony Johnson could show the police he had lied. Anthony Johnson, emerging from the lavatory at twenty to twelve, had seen him creeping up the stairs in the dark.

He could, of course, say he had merely been down to deposit rubbish in the dustbin. He? At that hour? In his overcoat? No, whatever he said, Anthony Johnson's testimony would be enough to draw their attention to him. And naturally Anthony Johnson would tell them. By now they would know, would perhaps be waiting for him at 142 Trinity Road.

Arthur went back there because he had nowhere else to go. No police car, no policeman in the hall. He stood in the hall, listening, wondering if they were up there on the top landing. A door above him crashed for all the world as if Jonathan Dean were back. And he was. Arthur stared. Jonathan Dean was coming downstairs with that black man and Anthony Johnson.

He managed to say good evening. Winston Mervyn said good evening back, but Jonathan Dean said nothing. He was drunk perhaps. He looked drunk, leaning on Mervyn's arm, his face grey and puffy. They went out into the street. Anthony Johnson said, "I'll be with you in a minute," and turned away to the hall table where he began sifting through the heap of letters Arthur hadn't felt capable of arranging methodically that morning. Arthur couldn't leave him to it and go upstairs. He edged along the hall almost shyly, but his heart was pounding with terror.

Anthony Johnson was looking annoyed. He said rather absently to Arthur, "An awful thing, this murder."

Arthur found a voice, a husky weak voice that came from somewhere in the back of his neck. "Have the police—have they interviewed you?"

And now Anthony Johnson turned round to face him, his blue eyes very penetrating. "No, they haven't, oddly enough. I'm surprised, because I do have things to tell them."

"I see." Arthur could hear his own voice as strange, as throaty. "Will you—will you go and tell them off your own bat, as it were?"

"I shouldn't think so. They can come to me if they want me. I don't see myself as the instrument of justice or the means of shutting a man up for life. Except, maybe, in very special circumstances. I mean, if an injury were done to me or mine, for instance."

Arthur nodded. Relief caused sweat to break over him, flushing him with heat. Anthony Johnson's meaning was unmistakable, hardly veiled, and as if to reinforce it, as Arthur began to walk away, he called:

"Mr. Johnson?"

"Yes?"

"I've been meaning to thank you for that note you left me. It was weeks ago but we don't seem to have met since. You remember? When you opened my letter by mistake?"

"Yes."

"It was thoughtful of you to leave that note." Anthony Johnson's voice was very gentle now, very considerate. Was he imagining the hint of menace that underlay it or was that menace really there? "I wouldn't like you to think I'd bear a grudge. It wasn't as if it was a very personal letter."

"Oh no," Arthur stammered. "No, indeed. A personal letter— that would be a dreadful intrusion." He cleared his throat. "An injury," he said.

15

Brian Kotowsky was the only son of Polish Jews, now dead, who had emigrated to this country in the nineteen thirties. Stanley Caspian told Arthur that Jonathan Dean and Vesta's brother were the only close associates Brian had had, and they had been, therefore, closely questioned by the police as to his possible hiding place. The brother-in-law remembered hearing of an aunt of Brian's, his mother's sister, who lived in Brighton, but when the police went to her house they found that she had been in hospital for a minor operation since the day before Vesta's death.

"I don't know." By this Arthur meant he didn't know how Stanley could know so much. Some grass-roots system, perhaps, that had often proved reliable in the past.

"He'll have skipped off to South America," said Stanley, jabbing full stops into Li-li Chan's rent book. "They must have had a fortune stashed away, him and her, considering they were both working and not paying me more than a poxy fourteen quid a week for that flat."

"Two rooms," said Arthur absently.

"A two-roomed flat with fridge and immersion heater. Cheap at the price. Put the kettle on, me old Arthur. Mrs. Caspian's sister's mother-in-law's got a pal who knows a chap that keeps a paper shop up West Hampstead, West End Lane, and he told the pal he'd been helping the police in their enquiries on account of Kotowsky going in there Wednesday morning to get some fags and a paper. Identified him, this paper-shop chap did, from photos. And he's the last living soul to have set eyes on him. Have a bit of pie?"

"No, thank you," said Arthur.

"God knows what he was doing in Hampstead. It's more than I can understand, a chap killing his own wife, me and Mrs. Caspian having been a pair of real lovebirds all our married life. A cream passionate is what they call it. Thank God it wasn't under my roof. There's nothing like that to give a place a bad name. What's worrying me is when I'll be able to relet the flat. I can't afford to take a drop in my income at this juncture, I can tell you."

"I shouldn't wonder," said Arthur with malice, "if the authorities don't seal it up for months and months. And now, if I might have my little envelope?"

In his pocket was another, mauve-grey, postmarked Bristol, which he had picked up from the doormat ten minutes before. Who could have suspected that she would write again, having been turned down, or apparently turned down, and send a letter to arrive on a Saturday? However, because Stanley Caspian was already parking his car at the kerb, he had snatched it up. Now he wondered why, for he intended no further revenge on Anthony Johnson. Far from it. Just as Anthony Johnson had forgiven him for opening that letter from the council, so he would forgive Anthony Johnson for that act of destruction by fire. *Must* forgive him, because now he was entirely in Anthony Johnson's power.

Dropping the Bristol letter on his kitchen table, Arthur forced himself to think clearly. Anthony Johnson had said plainly that he wouldn't pardon the theft of a personal letter. No letter could be more personal than last Tuesday's. Therefore, he must never know that Arthur had taken it. He would surely go to the police and tell what he had seen if he suspected Arthur of interfering with his correspondence. So Anthony Johnson must have this letter. But what if H. mentioned in it that she had written before? Arthur plugged in his electric kettle. The envelope flap reacted obediently to the jet of steam and curled easily away. With extreme care, he took out the sheet of flimsy.

Darling Tony, Why haven't I heard from you? I couldn't believe it when the post brought me nothing from you. Letters don't go astray, do they? But the alternative is that you didn't want to write, that you're angry with me, making me wait now as I made you wait in the past. Or is it that you need time to think in, to make plans for where we shall live and so on? I see you may need time to adjust to a new life and disrupt the new one you have already made. But if you need weeks, if you want to wait till your term ends, can't you understand that I'll understand? I'm so entirely yours now, Tony, that I'll do anything you ask. Only don't let me endure suspense, don't leave me in fear.

But there isn't any real need to be frightened, is there? I know you'll write. Is it possible that someone living in your house would take your letters by mistake. Surely, no one who did that would keep a letter like mine, a true love letter. And yet I hope and hope this is what happened. Or that this murder in your street I've read about in the newspapers has somehow made the police take people's post.

Because I have to believe you didn't get my letter, I'll repeat what I said in it, that I'll leave Roger and come to you whenever you like. Your most devoted and loving, H.

Arthur read it several times. He wondered at the emotion conveyed in it. Strange that anyone could put such exaggerations, such drama, on paper. But her guesswork was correct. Her previous letter had been purloined by someone living in the house, and therefore Anthony Johnson must no more receive this one than he had received the last. He must never be allowed to receive any letter in a mauve-grey envelope, postmarked Bristol. . . .

~~~~~~~~

When nothing had arrived from Helen by the weekend, Anthony's attitude towards her wavered between resentful anger and the more reasonable feeling that her letter had got lost in the post. She would, in any case, write again next week. It brought him a small, bitter pleasure to think she might have written to say she had made up her mind in his favour. How ironical if it were that letter which had got lost and she now be wondering if he were paying her back in her own coin. But he didn't really think she would have decided for him. The likeliest answer was that she had written with her usual ambivalence, given the letter to some colleague or friend to post, and it lay even now in that friend's pocket or handbag.

On Saturday night he phoned Linthea, but she was out and Leroy's sitter answered. However, on Sunday evening she was free and Anthony was invited to the flat in Brasenose Avenue.

The Sunday newspapers all had photographs of Brian Kotowsky, dog-faced Brian with his wild hair and his unhappy eyes. POLICE MOUNT MASSIVE SEARCH FOR VESTA'S HUSBAND. She was Vesta now to everyone, a household word, her Christian name on the lips of strangers enough to summon up immediate images of violence, terror, passion, death. But, keeping their options open, the less genteel of the Sundays also carried whole page spread stories entitled in one case, WAS VESTA KENBOURNE KILLER'S VICTIM? and in another, echoing poor Brian's own words, KENBOURNE KILLER STRIKES AGAIN?

Linthea, in the kitchen making Chicken Maryland, talked about the murder practically, logically, like a character in a detective story. "If Brian Kotowsky did kill her, he can't have gone straight to find this Dean, because he left your house at a quarter to eleven and she didn't leave the Grand Duke till ten minutes later. So they're saying he hung about in the street on a freezing cold night on the chance she'd come that way and at that time. When she did come they didn't go home to quarrel but quarrelled in a pitch-black mews where he killed her. And that's ridiculous."

"We don't know what they're saying."

"The police always think murdered wives have been murdered by their husbands, and considering what I see in my work every day almost, I know why."

He thought how Helen would have spoken of it, with intuition, using her rich imagination to clothe that night and the players in its drama. But Linthea looked coolly and prosaically at things as he did. Linthea had more in common with him than Helen had. Strange that the girl gifted with the delicate perception, the passionate imagination, should look so cool and fair, the calm and practical one so exotic. Tonight Linthea's long black hair hung loose down her back. She wore a heavy gold chain about her neck which threw a yellow gleam up against her throat and chin. He wondered about that dead husband of hers and whether she now lived a celibate life.

Later, when they had eaten and she had exhausted the subject of the Kotowskys, completed her analysis of times and circumstances and likelihood, he felt an overpowering urge to confide in her about Helen. But that brought him back to where he had been once before. Can you, if you want to make love to a woman, confess to her your present, strong, and angry love for another woman? Not certainly, with her son in the room, pressing you to a game of Scrabble.

"You're keeping him up late," he said at last.

"He's on half-term. No school tomorrow, no work for me." She had a merry laugh, evoked by very little, as some West Indians have. "Scrabble's good for him, he can't spell at all. How will you grow up," she said, hugging the boy, "to be a big important doctor like Anthony if you can't spell?"

So they played Scrabble till midnight when Leroy went to bed and Linthea said very directly, "I shall send you home now, Anthony. You must be fresh for your psychopaths in the morning."

He didn't feel very fresh on Tuesday morning because he had awakened at four and been unable to sleep again. All day he wondered if a letter would be waiting for him when he got home, though he refused to give way to the impulse that urged him to go home early and find out. But when he returned at five there was no letter. No post had come that day for the occupants of 142 Trinity Road and the table was bare. So, on the following morning, beginning now to feel real anxiety, he waited at home until the post came, and at nine he took it in himself. Two letters, one for Li-li, one for Winston. It was now two whole weeks since he had heard from Helen.

Two of her letters couldn't have gone astray. He considered breaking her rule and phoning her at work. She was assistant to the curator of a marine art museum. But why give her what she wanted, a lover content to hang on, playing the *amour courtois* game, while she gave him nothing? No, he wouldn't phone. And maybe he wouldn't phone on the last Wednesday of the month either. By that time, anyway, he might have managed to console himself. Linthea, he thought, Linthea who had no ties, who lived in and worked for a society he understood, who wasn't effete with poetry and dream and metaphor and a jellylike sensitivity that melts at a hard touch. Above all, this mustn't affect his thesis. He had begun to write it in earnest and it was going well. Now, having dealt in depth with the findings of various psychometric tests, he wrote:

In the survey it was suggested that the majority of psychopaths feared their own aggression and were as guilt- and anxiety-ridden about their acts as were the normal subjects. In their manner of relating to female and authority figures, a greater disturbance was found in psychopaths than in non-psychopaths, but whereas more guilt feelings were present in the former, further analysis shows that the guilt feelings of psychopaths were indicative rather of their difficult and disagreeable situation than of true remorse. The psychopath, when offered a choice between selfish forms of conduct and those which seem self-denying and are therefore socially acceptable, may be shrewd enough to choose the latter. When obliged to be guided solely by his own judgment, his choice is directed primarily by personal need. . . .

A tap on the door, discreet and somehow insinuating, interrupted Anthony. Arthur Johnson stood outside, dressed as usual in one of his silver-sheened suits and a shirt as white as that in a detergent commercial. He gave a small, deprecating cough.

"I do most sincerely apologise for this intrusion, but I have to trouble you about the little matter of the rent. Your—er, first weekly payment in advance falls due tomorrow."

"Oh, sure," said Anthony. "Will a cheque do?"

"Admirably, admirably."

While Anthony hunted out his chequebook which was sandwiched between Sokolov's *The Conditioned Reflex* and Stein's *Role of Pleasure in Behaviour*, Arthur Johnson, in a finicky manner, waved at him a small red rent book and a brown envelope on which was printed with a touching attention to detail: Mr. Anthony Johnson, Room 2, 142 Trinity Road, London W15 6HD.

"If you would be good enough to place your cheque inside your rent book each Friday and the book inside this little envelope? Then I will either collect it or you may leave it on the hall table."

Anthony nodded, wrote his cheque.

"Thank goodness, the police have ceased to trouble us."

"They haven't troubled me at all yet," said Anthony.

"Of course, there can be no doubt in anyone's mind that Mr. Kotowsky is guilty. He's known to be in South America but he will be extradited."

"Oh, rubbish," said Anthony rather more roughly than he intended. "And there's plenty of doubt in my mind. I don't believe for a moment he did it."

Arthur had been rather perturbed during the previous week to observe that on two mornings the post had been taken in by someone else. But that hadn't happened since Saturday—thanks to his watching from his living-room window for the postman to appear round the corner of Camera Street, and taking care to be down in the hall in good time. In any case, no further mauve-grey envelopes had arrived. The woman wouldn't write again. She had now been twice rebuffed and she wouldn't risk a further snub. Tuesday, November 19, and Wednesday, November 20, went by. Those were crucial days, but they brought Anthony Johnson only a letter from York from his mother. Arthur felt more relaxed and peaceful than he had done since the night of November 5, although it gave him a certain bitterness to notice, now when it was too late and unimportant, that twice this week already no light had fallen from the window of Room 2 on to the courtyard in the evenings.

Friday, November 22, dawned cold and wet. Arthur saw Anthony Johnson leave the house at eight-thirty and Winston Mervyn follow him five minutes later. Then Li-li Chan emerged. She stood at the front gate under a red pagoda umbrella, scanning the cars that turned into Trinity Road from Magdalen Hill. Then the front door slammed with a Dean-like crash and Arthur heard her platform soles clumping up the stairs. He opened his door and put it on the latch.

Li-li was on the phone.

"You say you come at eight-thirty. You are oversleeping? Why don't you buy alarm clock? I am late for my work. You would not oversleep if I sleep with you?" Arthur clicked his tongue at that one. "Perhaps I will, perhaps I won't. Of course I love you. Now come quick before I get sack from my job."

It was five to nine before the car came for her, an ancient blue van this time. Arthur went down to take in the post. There was nothing on the mat, so presumably the postman hadn't yet come. But as he turned back into the hall, he saw that the table which on the previous night had been bare even of vouchers, now held a pile of envelopes. The post must have come early and while he was listening to Li-li's phone conversation. She had taken it in herself.

His own new Barclaycard, two circulars for Winston Mervyn and—unbelievable but real—a mauve-grey envelope postmarked Bristol. She had written again. Was there no stopping her? Arthur held the envelope in his fingertips, held it at arm's length, as if it might explode. Well, he had decided no Bristol letter must ever be allowed to reach Anthony Johnson and that decision should stand. Better burn the thing immediately as he had burned the last. And yet . . . A thrill of fear touched him. Li-li had taken that letter in, might or might not have noticed it. But how could he be sure she hadn't? If Anthony Johnson began to wonder why no letter had come for him for three weeks and started asking around—following up, in fact, H's suggestion, though it had never been communicated to him—then Li-li would remember.

Again he steamed open the envelope.

Darling Tony, What have I done? Why have you rejected me without a word? You begged me to make up my mind and let you know as soon as I could. I did let you know by the Tuesday. I told you I was willing to leave Roger as soon as I heard from you and that I'd come to you. That was November 5 and now it's November 21. Please tell me what I did and where I went wrong. Is it because I said I couldn't promise to love you for ever? God knows, I've wished a thousand times I'd never written those words. Or is it because I said I hadn't told Roger? I would have told him, you must believe me, as soon as I'd heard from you.

I think I've lost you. In so far as I can think rationally at all, I think I shall never see you again. Tony, you would have pity on

me if you knew what black despair I feel, as if I can't go on an-
other day. I would even come to you, only I'm terrified of your
anger. You said there are other women in the world. I am afraid
to come and find you with another girl. It would kill me. You
said I was the only woman you had ever felt real passion for,
apart from wanting them as friends or to sleep with. You said
you thought "in love" was an old-fashioned meaningless expres-
sion, but you understood it at last because you were in love with
me. These feelings can't have been destroyed because I wrote
tactless silly things in my first letter. Or weren't they ever sin-
cere?

Roger has gone to Scotland on business. He's to be there at
least a fortnight and wanted me to go with him, only I can't get
time off from work till next Wednesday. Tony, while I'm alone
here, please will you phone me at home? At any time during the
weekend—I won't leave the house—or next week in the evenings.
I beg you to. If I ever meant anything to you in the past, if only
for what we once were to each other, I beg you to phone me. If
it's only to say you don't want me, you've changed your mind, I
want to hear you saying it. Don't be so cruel as to let me wait by
the phone all the weekend. I can take it—I think—if you say
you've changed. What I can't take is this awful silence.

But, Tony, if you don't phone, and I have to face the possi-
bility that you won't, I shan't write again. I don't know what I
shall do, but what little pride I have left will keep me from
throwing myself at you. So whatever happens now, this is my
last letter. H.

That, Arthur thought, rereading the last sentence, was at any
rate something to be thankful for. But if Anthony Johnson saw
this letter he'd be on the phone at once, tonight. And in their
conversation it would all come out, the dates she'd written and
the things she'd written. Yet Anthony Johnson must see this letter because Li-li Chan had already seen it.

By now it was almost twenty past nine. Arthur considered not
going to work, phoning Mr. Grainger and saying he'd got this
gastric bug that was going about. He seemed to see Auntie
Gracie loom before him, shaking her head at his deceit and his
cowardice. Besides, he'd have to go back tomorrow or the next

day. Shivering as if he were really ill, he dragged on his raincoat and took his umbrella from the rack in the hall. What to do with H's letter? Take it to work and try to think of some solution. He could come home at lunchtime, anyway, in good time to restore it if he could find no alternative but to deliver it and himself into Anthony Johnson's hands.

He was late, of course, late for the first time in years. Drizzle speckled the office window, then rain gushed in sheets against the glass. In a wretched state that was intensely nervous and at the same time apathetic, Arthur opened Grainger's post, though he felt he never wanted to see another envelope as long as he lived. The handwriting of potential customers who wanted roofs retiled and central heating installed danced before his eyes. He typed two replies, full of errors, but at last there was nothing for it but to take H's letter out of his briefcase and scrutinise it once more.

Should he take a chance on Li-li's having failed to notice it? The chances were she hadn't noticed it among so much other stuff. Since there seemed no alternative, this was a risk he would have to take. Destroy the letter now and hope Anthony Johnson either wouldn't bother to ask her or that she wouldn't remember. He had closed his fist over the two sheets of flimsy paper when he realised, with a new terror, that even if Anthony Johnson didn't get this latest of H's letters, he would still discover the injury that had been done him. For on Wednesday, November 27, next Wednesday, the last Wednesday in the month, he would phone H as he always did and the whole thing would come out.

⁓⁓⁓⁓⁓

Arthur ground two sheets of paper into his typewriter and struggled with a reply to a Mr. P. Coleman, who wanted Grainger's advice on the conversion of his nineteenth-century coachhouse into a dwelling for his mother-in-law. H's letter would have to go back to 142 Trinity Road by one and it was eleven now. He'd brazen it out, that was all. He'd deny in his most severe manner ever having touched Anthony Johnson's correspondence. Useless to keep turning things over in his mind like this when there was no help for it. He glanced at the sheet on which he was typing and saw he had put an H instead of a P before Coleman and "convict" instead of "convert." The paper was torn out and a fresh sheet inserted. Anthony Johnson would go at once to the police. The police would stop hunting for Brian Kotowsky and start thinking seriously about Arthur Johnson, who never went out at night but who had been out that night; who was a resident of Kenbourne Vale at the time of the murder of Maureen Cowan and at the time of the murder of Bridget O'Neill; who had unaccountably lied to them. . . . He flexed his hands to try and prevent their trembling.

A mammoth effort, a mammoth concentration, and a passable letter advising Mr. Coleman to consult a certain firm of Kenbourne Vale architects had been achieved. But as soon as he had done it and read it through, it struck him that if this reply came to the notice of Mr. Grainger he would be very displeased indeed. Mr. Grainger would expect him, while possibly mentioning the architects, to suggest that Grainger's themselves would be happy to carry out the work. The displeasure of the whole world, of everyone who mattered, loomed before him. He gave a shuddering sigh. Another, and very different, letter must be composed.

Fresh sheets of paper were in the machine before Arthur realized the significance of the words he had spoken under his breath. Another, and very different, letter must be composed. . . .

16

For her letters H always used the same flimsy paper Grainger's used for their carbon copies. And she used a similar typewriter to Arthur's. Suppose he himself were to type a letter to Anthony Johnson and insert it in that mauve-grey envelope? The envelope would be the original one, the postmark and its date correct, and it could be placed on the hall table in good time for Anthony Johnson to find it. Only the contents would be different.

Arthur, who had spent half a day composing with fear and extreme care that note of apology, was appalled by the magnitude and the danger of the task. And yet the letter wouldn't have to be a long one. His purpose, already half formulated, was to make it as short as possible. He could imitate H's hysterical style—he had seen enough of it—and make the sort of errors she made, not depressing that key properly so that it made an eight instead of an apostrophe, depressing this one too long so that the second as well as the initial letter came out as upper case. And he could make the H with his own blue-black ballpoint pen.

He put two sheets of flimsy into the typewriter. The date first: November 21, and the O of November a capital as well as the N. *Darling Tony*—no, she wouldn't call him darling for the kind of letter he meant to write. What would she call him? The only personal letters Arthur had written in his whole life were to a certain cousin of Auntie Gracie's who had sent him five shilling postal orders on his birthdays. *Dear Uncle Alfred, Thank you very much for the postal order. I am going to save the money up in my money box. I had a nice birthday. Auntie Gracie gave me a new school blazer. With love from Arthur.* Dear Tony? In the end, not having the least idea whether people ever wrote that way, Arthur typed *Tony*. Just *Tony*.

How to begin? She was always asking him to forgive her. *Forgive me*. That was good, convincing. *I'm sorry*, he went on, taking care that an eight instead of an apostrophe appeared, *not to have written to you before as I promised*. Why hadn't she written? *I knew you would be angry if I said I couldn't make up my mind*. Good, he was doing well. But he must get on to the nub of it. *I have made it up now and I am going to stay with Roger. I am his wife and it is my duty to stay with him*. Arthur didn't like that much, it wasn't H's style, but he couldn't better it and still make her say what he meant her to say. There ought to be some love stuff. He racked his brains for something from the television or from one of those old films. *I never really loved you. It was just infatuation*. Now for the most important thing, the point of writing this letter that was primarily designed to put an end to all further communication between H and Anthony Johnson.

Barry loafed in just before one to say he had had his lunch and would be around to answer the phone while Arthur was out. It was still teeming with rain. Arthur put up his umbrella and set off for Trinity Road via the mews. He passed the spot where he had strangled Vesta Kotowsky, feeling a tickle of nostalgia and a fretful resentment against a society which had given him the need to commit such acts yet would condemn him with loathing for yielding to them.

The house was empty. Nothing on the table had been disturbed. Arthur checked that the flap of the mauve-grey envelope was securely gummed down, and then he placed it in the very centre of the glossy mahogany table.

~~~~~~~~~~

The house was semidetached, with the uncluttered lines of sixties building, of pale red bricks with big windows to let in ample light. The family who had lived there since it was new had planted each January in its front garden their Christmas trees, and these Norway spruces, ten of them, stood in a row, each one a little taller than its predecessor. Anthony, as he left the house with Winston, thought of Helen and the delight she would have taken in those Christmas trees, seeing in their arrangement, the almost ritualistic placing of them, evidence of domestic harmony, quietude, and a sense of permanent futurity.

The street was very quiet, a cul-de-sac. Children could play there in safety. But there were no children playing now, for it was dark, dark as midnight at six o'clock.

"What d'you think?" said Winston.

"Very nice, if you've got twenty thousand pounds. But you'll have to get married. It's no place for a bachelor. You must get married, have children, and with luck you'll be able to plant at least forty more Christmas trees."

"Do I detect a note of sarcasm?"

"Sorry," said Anthony. Viewing the house had made him bitter. It wasn't his ideal, too bourgeois, too dull, too sheltered, and yet—could you find a better place in which to build a marriage and raise a family? Relationships are hard to come by, and one woman may make a man very discriminating, very selective. He saw his youth wasted in hanging after Helen, their dream children vanishing in their dream mother's vacillations.

Winston said, "I think I shall buy it. I shall come and live here among the nobs." He pointed as they turned the corner to a grander street. "Caspian lives in one of those minimansions, and all made out of grinding our faces."

They walked towards the K.12 stop. A thin, cold drizzle was falling. It laid a slimy sheen on pavements and on the darker tarmac of the roadway, which threw back glittering yellow and red reflections of lamps. The neighbourhood changed abruptly as London neighbourhoods do. Once again they were among the tenements, the dispirited rows of terraced cottages without gardens or fences, the corner shops, the new housing blocks.

"You can always tell council flats by the smallness of their windows," said Anthony. "Have you noticed?"

"And their hideous design. It comes of giving second-rate architects a chance to experiment on people who can't afford to refuse."

"Unlike lucky you."

"In a filthy temper tonight, aren't you? Excuse me, I'm going in here to get a paper."

Anthony waited at the door. What was happening to him that

he could be rude and resentful to this new friend he liked so much? He stood in the now fast-falling rain, feeling depression settle on him. Friday night, Friday, November 22. He had to get through another five days of this, five days till the last Wednesday of the month. But then he would phone her, certainly he would. He thought of her face that he hadn't seen for two months. It appeared before his eyes like a ghost face in mist, delicate, sensitive, contrite, wistful. The last time he had made love to her—he remembered it now, her eyes open and watching his eyes, her smile that had nothing to do with amusement. To have that again, even impermanently, even deferred, wasn't it worth sacrificing his pride for that, his ideal of himself as strong and decisive, for that? Yes, on Wednesday he would beg and persuade all over again, he would begin again. . . .

Winston came out of the shop, holding the paper up, reading the front page. He came up to Anthony, thrust the paper at him. "Look."

The first thing Anthony saw was the photograph of Brian, the uncompromising passport photograph that had appeared so many times already, day after day, in every newspaper. The mop of hair, the wizened yet flaccid face, the eyes that ever seemed to implore, ever to irritate with their silliness. First the picture, then the headline: VESTA'S HUSBAND FOUND DROWNED. The account beneath those huge black letters was brief.

The body of a man washed up on the beach at Hastings, Sussex, was today identified as that of Brian Kotowsky, 38, husband of Vesta Kotowsky, strangled on Guy Fawkes Day in Kenbourne Vale, West London. Mr. Kotowsky had been missing since the day following his wife's death.

Mr. Kotowsky, an antique dealer, of Trinity Road, Kenbourne Vale, was known to have relatives in Brighton.

His aunt, Mrs. Janina Shaw, said today that she had not seen her nephew for nine years.

"We were once very close," she said. "We lost touch when Brian married. I cannot say if my nephew visited my house prior to his death as I have been ill in hospital."

An inquest will be held.

Anthony looked at Winston. Winston shrugged, his face closed and expressionless. The rain fell onto the newspaper, darkening it with great heavy splashes.

On the way home they hardly spoke. With a kind of delicacy but without communicating that delicacy to each other, they avoided the mews and walked to Trinity Road by the long way round. Then Winston said:

"I shouldn't have let him go out. I should have dissuaded him and put him to bed and then none of this would have happened."

"No one is responsible for another adult person."

"Can you define an adult person?" said Winston. "It isn't a matter of years."

Anthony said no more. Entering the hall, he remembered meeting Brian there for the first time. Brian had been sitting on the stairs doing up his shoelaces and he had come up to him and said, "Mr. Johnson, I presume?" Now he was dead, had walked out into the wintry sea until he drowned. He heard Winston say, as from a long way off, that he had a date at seven-thirty, that he must hurry.

"And I must do some work. Have a good time."

"I'll try. But I wish I hadn't seen a paper till tomorrow morning."

Winston set his foot on the bottom stair, then, having glanced over the banisters, turned and walked up to the table. He picked up three envelopes. "Now I've decided on my house, I must remember to tell these agents to stop sending me stuff." He handed a fourth envelope to Anthony, a mauve-grey one with a Bristol postmark. "Here's one for you," he said.

~~~~~~~~~

At last, after so long, she had written. To say she wanted his patience a little longer? That she had been ill? Or, wonder of wonders, that she was coming to him? He unlocked his door and kicked on the switch of the electric fire. A single thumb thrust split open the flap of the envelope. He pulled out the sheet of flimsy. Just one sheet? That must mean she had hardly anything to say, that she had settled in his favour. On the brink of a happy upheaval of his life, of consummation, he read it.

Tony, Forgive me. I'm sorry not to have written to you before as I promised. I knew you would be angry if I said I couldn't make up my mind. I have made it up now and I am going to stay with Roger. I am his wife and it is my duty to stay with him.

I never really loved you. It was just infatuation. You must forget me and it will soon be as if you hadn't known me.

Do not phone me. You mustn't try to get in touch with me at all. Not ever. Roger will be angry if you do. So remember, this is final. I shall not see you again and you must not contact me. H.

Anthony read it again because at first he simply couldn't believe it. It was as if a letter for someone else and written by someone else had got into one of those envelopes whose colour and shape and texture had always held a magic of their own. This—this obscenity—couldn't be intended for him, couldn't have been written by her to him. And yet it had been. Her typewriter had been used, those distinctive errors were hers. He read it a third time, and now rage began to conquer disbelief. How dare she write such hideous, cliché-ridden rubbish to *him?* How dare she keep him waiting three weeks and then write this? The language appalled him almost as much as the sentiments it expressed. Her duty to stay with Roger! And then that lonelyhearts novelette word "infatuation." "Contact" too—journalese for approach or communicate. He examined the letter, analysing it, as if close scrutiny of semantics could keep him from facing the pain of it.

The truth flashed upon him. Of course. She had begun it and the remainder had been dictated by Roger. Instead of serving to pacify him, this realisation only made him angrier. She had confessed to Roger and he had compelled her to write like this. But what sort of a woman was it who would let a man take her over to that extent? And when did she think she was living, she who was self-supporting and had the franchise and was strong and healthy? A hundred years ago? A deep humiliation enclosed him as he imagined them composing that letter in concert, the woman abject and grateful for forgiveness, the man domineering, relegating him, Anthony, to the status of some gigolo.

"You give that presumptuous devil his marching orders. Let him know whose wife you are and where your duty lies. And put in something about not contacting you if he values his skin. For God's sake, Helen, make him see it's final. . . ."

Final.

He screwed the letter up, then unscrewed it and tore it into tiny shreds so that the temptation to read it again was removed.

17

The news of Brian Kotowsky's death reached Arthur at nine o'clock that night by way of the television. The announcer didn't say much about it, only that a drowned corpse had been identified and that there would be an inquest. But Arthur was satisfied. He had never even considered that honourable promptings of conscience might bring him qualms when Brian was tried for Vesta's murder. Brian Kotowsky was nothing to him, his indifference towards the dead man tempered only by a natural dislike of someone who got drunk and was noisy. But Kotowsky might have been acquitted. Nothing could now acquit him. His self-dealt death marked him as plainly a murderer as any confession or any trial could have done. The police would consider the case as closed.

He slightly regretted his forgery of the morning. So much of his life had been ruined by terror, so much of his time wasted by gruelling anxiety. All of it in vain. But he consoled himself with the thought that, at the time, he had had no choice. Undoubtedly, Kotowsky's death hadn't appeared in the early editions of the evening papers so, even if he had bought one, he still wouldn't have known in time to avoid the substitution of the letter. But now, if Anthony Johnson were to find him out, there was no damaging action he could take. The police had a culprit, dead and speechless.

And so to get on with the business of living. Arthur watched a very old film about the building of the Suez Canal, starring Loretta Young as the Empress Eugénie and Tyrone Power as de Lesseps, till eleven. He enjoyed it very much, having seen it before with Auntie Gracie when he was thirteen. Those were the days. In euphoric mood, he really thought they had been. Saturday tomorrow. The new attendant at the launderette was Mr. Grainger's nephew's wife, earning a bit of pin money, and he thought he could safely leave his washing with her while he went to the shops. Maybe he'd treat himself to a duck for Sunday by way of celebration.

~~~~~~~~~~

There are ways and ways of ending a love affair. Anthony thought of the ways he had ended with girls in the past and the ways they had ended with him. Cool discussions, rows, pseudo-noble renunciations, cheerful let's-call-it-a-day farewells. But it had never been Helen's way. No one had rid herself of him with a curt note. And yet any of those other girls would have been more justified in doing so, for he had claimed to love none of them and offered none of them permanency. A last meeting he could have taken, a final explanation from her or even an honest letter, inviting him to phone her for a last talk. What he had received was more than he could take and he refused it. There still remained the last Wednesday of the month. Tomorrow. He would ask Linthea for the use of her phone so that there wouldn't be that hassle with the change. And Helen should learn she couldn't dismiss him as if he were some guy she'd picked up and spent a couple of nights with.

Leroy was still at school when he called at Linthea's on his way home from college. "You're welcome," she said, "but I have to go out around eight, so when you've done your phoning, would you sit with Leroy for an hour or two?"

This wasn't exactly what Anthony had envisaged. He had seen himself needing a little comfort after speaking his mind to Helen. On the other hand, this way Linthea wouldn't have to know whom he was phoning and why. And there would be plenty of time later in the week, next week, the week after, for consolation. All the time in the world . . .

Linthea was ready to go out when he got there and Leroy was playing Monopoly in his bedroom with Steve and David. Because it was still only ten to eight, Anthony passed the time by

reading the evening paper's account of the inquest on Brian Kotowsky. Evidence was given of the murder of Brian's wife three
weeks before, of his disappearance but not a hint was breathed
that Brian might have been responsible for that murder. The
body had been in the sea for a fortnight and identification had
been difficult. No alcohol had been present, but the cumulative
effects of alcohol were found in the arteries and the liver. The
verdict, in the absence of any suicide note or prior-to-death ad-
mission of unhappiness on Brian's part, was one of misadventure.
In a separate paragraph Chief Superintendent Howard Fortune,
head of Kenbourne Vale C.I.D., was quoted as saying simply,
"I have no comment to make at this stage."

Eight o'clock. He would give it till ten past. Steve and David
went home, and Anthony talked to Leroy, telling him stories
about a children's home where he had once worked and where
the boys had got out of the windows by night and gone off to
steal cars. Leroy was entranced, but Anthony's heart wasn't in
it. At eight-fifteen he put the television on, gave Leroy milk and
biscuits and shut himself up in Linthea's bedroom where she had
a phone extension.

He dialled the Bristol number and it began to ring. When it
had rung twelve times he knew she wasn't going to answer.
Would she, after all there had been between them, just sit there
and let the phone ring? She must know it was he. He dialled
again and again it rang unanswered. After a while he went back
to Leroy and tried to watch a quiz programme. Nine o'clock
came and he forgot all about sending Leroy off to bed as he had
promised. Again he dialled Helen's number. She had gone out,
he thought, guessing he would phone. That was how she intended to behave if he tried to "contact" her. And when Roger
was at home and the phone rang they would have arranged it so
that he answered. . . . He put the receiver back and sat with a
contented little boy who didn't get sent to bed until five minutes
before his mother came home with Winston Mervyn.

"I don't owe you anything for the call," said Anthony. "I
couldn't get through."

He went home soon after and lay on his bed, thinking of ways
to get in touch with Helen. He could, of course, go to her house.
He could go on Saturday, it was only two hours to Bristol in the

train. Roger would be there, but he wasn't afraid of Roger, his guns, and his rages. But Roger would be *there*, would possibly open the door to him. With Roger enraged and belligerent, Helen frightened and obedient according to what she had the effrontery to call her duty, what could he say? And nothing would be said at all, for Roger wouldn't admit him to the house.

He could phone her mother if he knew what her mother was called or where she lived. The sister and brother-in-law? They had hardly proved trustworthy in the past. In the end he fell into an uneasy sleep. When he awoke at seven it occurred to him that he could phone her at the museum. He had never done so before because of her absurd neurosis about Roger's all-seeing eye and all-hearing ear, but he'd do it now and to hell with Roger.

He had planned to spend the day in the British Museum library but it didn't much matter what time he got there. At nine he went out and bought a couple of cans of soup at Winter's in order to get some change. On the way back he passed Arthur Johnson in a silver-grey overcoat and carrying a briefcase, the acme of respectability. Arthur Johnson said good morning and that the weather was seasonable, to which Anthony agreed absently. A hundred and forty-two was quite empty, totally silent. The seasonableness of the weather was evinced by a high wind, and little spots of coloured light cast through the wine-red and sap-green glass danced on the hall floor.

He went upstairs to the phone and dialled. Peep-peep-peep, and in went the first of his money. A girl's voice but not hers.

"Frobisher Museum. Can I help you?"

"I want to speak to Helen Garvist."

"Who is that calling?"

"It's a personal call," said Anthony.

"I'm afraid I must have your name."

"Anthony Johnson."

She asked him to hold the line. After about a minute she was back. "I'm afraid Mrs. Garvist isn't here."

He hesitated, then said, "She must be there."

"I'm afraid not."

Then he understood. She would have come to the phone if he hadn't given his name, if he had insisted on anonymity. But because she didn't want to talk to him, was determined at any cost not to talk to him, she had got the girl to tell this lie.

"Let me speak to the curator," he said firmly.

"I'll see if he's available."

The pips started. Anthony put in more money.

"Norman Le Queux speaking," said a thin academic voice.

"I'm a friend of Mrs. Helen Garvist and I'm speaking from London. From a call box. I want to speak to Mrs. Garvist. It's very urgent."

"Mrs. Garvist is taking a fortnight of her annual leave, Mr. Johnson."

How readily the name came to him. . . . He had been forewarned. "In November? She can't be."

"I beg your pardon?"

"I'm sorry, but I don't believe you. She told you to say that, didn't she?"

There was an astonished silence. Then the curator said, "I think the sooner we terminate this conversation the better," and he put the receiver down.

Anthony sat on the stairs. It is very easy to become paranoid in certain situations, to believe that the whole world is against you. But what if the whole world, or those significant members of it, truly are against you? Why should Helen go away now in the cold tail end of the year? She would have mentioned something about it in her last letter if she had planned to go away. No, it wasn't paranoid, it was only feasible to believe that, wanting no more of him, she had asked Le Queux and the museum staff to deny her to a caller named Anthony Johnson. Of course they would co-operate if she said this was a man who was pestering her. . . .

~~~~~~~~~

"Kotowsky's being cremated today," said Stanley Caspian.

Arthur put the rent envelopes on the desk in front of him. "Locally?" he said.

"Up the cemetery. Don't suppose there'll be what you'd call a big turn-out. Mrs. Caspian says I ought to put in an appearance, but there are limits. Where did I put me bag of crisps, Arthur?"

"Here," said Arthur, producing it with distaste from where it had fallen into the wastepaper basket.

"Poxy sort of day for a funeral. Eleven-thirty, they're having it, I'm told. Still, I should worry. I'm laughing, Arthur, things are looking up. Two bits of good news I've got. One, the cops say I can relet Flat 1 at my convenience, which'll be next week."

"It could do with a paint. A face-lift, as you might say."

"So could you and me, me old Arthur, but it's not getting it any more than we are. I've no objection to the new tenant getting busy with a brush."

"May I know your other piece of good news?"

"Reckon you'll have to, but I don't know how you'll take it. Your rent's going up, Arthur. All perfectly legal and above board, so you needn't look like that. Up to four-fifty a year which'll be another two quid a week in that little envelope, if you please."

Arthur had feared this. He could afford it. He knew the Rent Act made provision for just such an increase in these hard times. But he wasn't going to let Stanley get away with it totally unscathed. "No doubt you're right," he said distantly, "but I shall naturally have to go into the matter in my own interest. When you let me have the new agreement it would be wise for my solicitors to look at it." As a parting shot he added, "I fear you won't find it easy letting those rooms. Two violent deaths, you know. People don't care for that sort of thing, it puts them off."

He took his envelope and went upstairs, his equilibrium which had prevailed, though declining, for a week, now shaken. He hoped that any prospective tenants of the Kotowskys' flat would come round while he was at home, in which case he would take care to let them know all. A gloomy day of thin fog and fine rain. Not enough rain, though, for his umbrella. The orange plastic bag of laundry in one hand, the shopping basket in the other, he set off for the launderette.

Mr. Grainger's nephew's wife promised to keep an eye on his washing and pleased Arthur by commenting favourably on the quality of his bed linen. He bought a Dover sole for lunch, a pound of sprouts, a piece of best end of neck for Sunday. The K.12 bus drew up outside the Waterlily and, on an impulse, Arthur got on it. It dropped him at the cemetery gates.

This was the old part, this end, a necropolis of little houses, the grey lichen-grown houses of the dead. Some years back a girl had been found dead in one of these tombs, a family vault. Arthur paused in front of the iron door which closed off the entrance to this cavern. He had been there before, had been inside, for the girl had been strangled and he had wondered if the police would regard her as the third of his victims, though he had been safe in those days with his white lady. Her murderer had been caught. He walked under the great statue of the winged victory, past the tomb of the Grand Duke who had given his name to the pub, on to the crematorium. The chapel door was closed. Arthur opened it diffidently.

A conversation seemed to be taking place inside, for what else can you call it when one man is speaking to one other? The man who was speaking was a clergyman and the man who was listening, sole member of that congregation, was Jonathan Dean. Brian Kotowsky had only one friend to mourn him. Music began to play, but it was Muzak really, as if the tape playing in a supermarket had suddenly taken a religious turn. The coffin, blanketed in purple baize, began to move, and silently the beige velvet curtains drew together. Brian Kotowsky, like Arthur's white lady, had gone to the fire.

Arthur slipped out. He didn't want to be seen. He walked back towards the gates along another path, much overgrown, this one, by brambles and the creeping ivy and long-leaved weeds the frost hadn't yet killed. Droplets of water clung to stone and trembled on leaf and twig. Presently he came to the red granite slab on which was engraved: ARTHUR LEOPOLD JOHNSON, 1855–1921, MARIA LILIAN JOHNSON, 1857–1918, BELOVED WIFE OF THE ABOVE, GRACE MARIA JOHNSON, 1888–1955, THEIR DAUGHTER. BLESSED ARE THE DEAD WHICH DIE IN THE LORD. No room for him there, no room for his mother, though perhaps she too was dead. Perhaps that was why she hadn't come to Auntie Gracie's funeral. . . .

In his best dark suit and new black tie, he had sat in the front room of the house in Magdalen Hill, reading the paper. The paper was full of some journalist's theorising about the Kenbourne Killer and his latest victim. He had read it while he waited for the mourners, Uncle Alfred who had sent him the birthday postal orders, the Winters, Beryl's mother, Mrs. Goodwin from next door. It was she who had told him of Auntie Gracie's death.

A cold Monday in March it had been. His bedroom was icy, but no one in his milieu and at that time thought of heating bedrooms. Auntie Gracie awakened him at seven-thirty—he never questioned why he should get up at seven-thirty when he only worked next door and didn't have to be there till half-past nine—awakened him and left for him in the cold bathroom a jug of hot water for shaving. Then into clean underwear because it was Monday.

"If you keep yourself clean, Arthur, you don't need clean underclothes more than once a week."

But a fresh white shirt each day because a shirt goes on top and shows. Downstairs to the kitchen where the boiler was alight and the table laid for one. Since he became a man Auntie Gracie had put away childish things for him. She ate her breakfast before he came down and waited on him because he was now master of the house. A bowl of cornflakes, one egg, two rashers of collar bacon, it was always the same. And she had been just the same that morning, her grey hair in tight curls from the new perm she hadn't yet combed out, dark skirt, lilac jumper, black and lilac crossover overall, slippers that were so hard and plain and unyielding that you would have thought them walking shoes.

"It looks like rain." As he emptied a plate she took it and washed it. Between washing, she stood at the window, studying the sky above the rooftops in Merton Street. "You'd better take your umbrella."

Once he had protested that he didn't need an umbrella to walk twenty yards through light rain or a hat to withstand ten minutes' chill or a scarf against the faintly falling snow. But now he knew better. By keeping silent he could avoid hearing the words that aroused in him impotent anger and shame: "And when you get ill like you were last time, I suppose you'll expect me to work myself into the ground nursing you and waiting on you."

So he kept silent and didn't even attempt to argue that he might have spent a further hour in bed rather than on a stool in front of the boiler reading the paper. She bustled about the house, calling to him at intervals, "Ten to nine, Arthur," "Nine o'clock, Arthur." When he left, allowing himself ten minutes to walk next door, she came to the front door with him and put up her cheek for a kiss. Arthur always remembered those kisses when, in his introspective moments, he reminded himself how happy their relationship had been. And he felt a savage anger against Beryl's mother for a comment she had once made.

"You give that boy your cheek like you were showing the doctor a boil on your neck, Gracie."

That morning he had kissed her in the usual way. Many times since he had wished he had allowed his lips to linger or had put an arm round her heavy shoulders. But thinking this way was a kind of fantasising, identifying with characters from films, for he had no idea how to kiss or embrace. And he blocked off the picture at this point because, after the image of that unimaginable closeness, came a frightening conclusion of the embrace, the only possible ending to it. . . .

At eleven, when he was doing Grainger's accounts in the room at the side of the works—no little cedarwood and glass office in those days—Mr. Grainger had walked in with Mrs. Goodwin. He could see them now, Mr. Grainger clearing his throat, Mrs. Goodwin with tears on her face. And then the words: "Passed away . . . her heart . . . fell down before my eyes . . . gone, Arthur. There was nothing anyone could do."

Someone had been in and laid her out. Arthur wouldn't let the undertakers take the body till the following day. He knew what was right. The first night after death you watched by the dead. He watched. He thought of all she had done for him and what she had been—mother, father, wife, counsellor, housekeeper, sole friend. The large-featured face, waxen and calm, lay against a clean white pillowcase. He yearned towards her, wanting her back—for what? To be better than he had been? To please her as he had never pleased her? To explain or ask her for explanation? He didn't think it was for any of those things, and he was afraid to touch her, afraid even to let one of his cold fingers rest against her colder cheek. The hammering in his head was strong and urgent.

Not for nearly six years had he been out alone at night. But at half-past nine he went out, leaving Auntie Gracie on her own.

He slipped through the passage into Merton Street and then he walked and walked, far away to a pub where they wouldn't know him—the Hospital Arms.

There he drank two brandies. A stretch of weed-grown bomb site separated the hospital from the embankment, the railway line, and the footbridge that crossed it. Arthur didn't need to cross the line. His way home was by way of the long lane that straggled through tenements and cottages to the High Street. But he went on to the bomb site and lingered among the rubble stacks until the girl came hurrying over the bridge.

Bridget O'Neill, twenty, student nurse. She screamed when she saw him, before he had even touched her, but there was no one in that empty wasteland to hear her. A train roared past, letting out its double-noted bray. She ran from him, tripped over a brick, and fell. With his bare hands he strangled her on the ground, and then he left her, returning through the dark ways to Magdalen Hill. Soon he slept, falling into a sleep almost as deep, though impermanent, as that which enclosed Auntie Gracie in her last bed.

He had never tended her grave. Thick grass grew above the sides of the slab, and her Christian name was obliterated by tendrils of ivy. Death surrounded him, cold, musty, mildewed death, not the warm kind he wanted. He knew he had begun to want it again, and frightened, wearied by this urge which only death itself could end, he went back to the bus, the launderette and the eternal cleaning of the flat.

~~~~~~~~~~

Love is the cure for love. Anthony knew that, whatever might happen between him and Linthea it could at best be a distraction. But what was wrong with distractions? His love for Helen had been deep, precious, special. It was absurd to suppose that that could be replaced at will. But many activities and many emotions go under the name of love, and almost any one of them will for a while divert the mind from the real, true, and perfect thing.

So he set off for Brasenose Avenue, if not a jolly, thriving wooer, at least a purposeful one. In his time he had received very few refusals. His thoughts, embittered, took a base turn.

Was it likely that a widow, lonely, older than himself, would turn him down? And when he rang the doorbell it was answered almost at once by Linthea herself who drew him without a word into the flat and threw her arms round his neck. Afterwards he was thankful he hadn't responded as he had wanted to. Perhaps, even at that moment, he sensed that this was a kiss of a happiness so great as to include any third party.

Winston was in the sitting room. They had been drinking champagne. Anthony stuck his bottle of Spanish Graves on top of the cupboard where it wouldn't be noticed.

"You can be the first to congratulate us," Winston said. "Well, not the first if you count Leroy."

"You're getting married." Anthony uttered it as a statement rather than a question.

"Saturday week," Linthea said, embracing him again. "Do come!"

"Of course he'll come," said Winston. "We'd have told you before, we decided a week ago, but we wanted to make sure it was all right with Leroy first."

"And was it?"

Winston laughed. "Fine, only when Linthea said she was marrying me he said he'd rather have had you."

So Anthony also had to laugh at that one and drink some champagne and listen to Winston's romantic, but not sentimental, account of how he had always wanted Linthea, had lost her when she married and had later pursued her half across the world in great hope. Helen had once quoted to Anthony that it is a bitter thing to look at happiness through another man's eyes. He told himself that her quotations and her whole Eng. Lit. bit bored him, she was as bad as Jonathan Dean, and then he went home to do more work on his thesis.

Though the psychopath may suffer from compulsive urges or an obsessional neurosis, his condition is related to a lowered state of cortical arousal and a chronic need for stimulation. He may therefore face the warring elements of a routine-driven life and an inability to tolerate routine in the absence of exciting stimuli. . . .

He broke off, unable to concentrate. This wasn't what he wanted to write. He wanted—needed—to do something he had never done before, write a letter to Helen.

18

He wouldn't send it to her home, that would be worse than useless. To the museum then? Although she hadn't a secretary, he remembered her telling him there was a girl who opened the incoming post for herself and Le Queux. Her mother would do if only he knew her mother's address. He tried to remember the names of friends she had spoken of when they were together. There must be someone to whom he could entrust a letter that was for her eyes only.

Rereading her old letters in search of a name, a clue, was a painful exercise. *Darling Tony, I knew I'd miss you but I didn't know how bad it would be. . . .* That was the one with the bit in it about an invitation to a dress show. If he'd known the name of the dress shop . . . The people she'd been to school with, to college with? He recalled only Christian names, Wendy, Margaret, Hilary. Suppose he wrote to her old college? The authorities would simply forward the letter to her home. Anyone would do that unless he put in a covering letter expressly directing them not to. And could he bring himself to do that? Perhaps he could, especially as the letter he intended to write wasn't going to be a humble plea.

He wrote it. Not simply, just like that, but draft after draft until he wondered if he was as mentally unstable as the sick people he studied. The final result dissatisfied him but he couldn't improve on it.

Dear Helen, I love you. I think I loved you from the first moment we met, and though I would give a lot to blot this feeling out and be free of you, I can't. You were my whole hope for the future and it was you who gave me a purpose for my life. But that's enough of me, I don't mean to go in for maudlin self-pity.

This letter is about you. You led me to believe you loved me in the same way. You told me you had never loved anyone the way you loved me and that Roger was nothing to you except an object of pity. You made love with me many times, many beautiful unforgettable times, and you are not—I can tell this, you know—the kind of woman who sleeps with a man for fun or diversion. You almost promised to come away and live with me. No, it was more than that. It was a firm promise, postponed only because you wanted more time.

Yet you have ditched me in such a cold peremptory way that even now I can hardly believe it. When I think of that last letter of yours it takes my breath away. I don't mean to reproach you for the pain you have caused me but to ask you what you think you are doing to yourself? Have you, in these past weeks, ever asked yourself what kind of a woman can live your sort of ambivalent life, pretending and lying to a husband and lover equally? What happens to that woman as she grows older and begins to lose any idea of what truth is? Life isn't worth living for someone who is a coward, a liar and has lost self-respect, particularly when she is sensitive as, God knows, you are.

Think about it. Don't think about me if you don't want to but think about the damage fear and woolly mindedness and that sort of confusion are going to do to whatever there is under that pretty exterior of yours.

If you want to see me I'll see you. But I won't commit myself to more than that now. I think I would be wilfully damaging my own self if I were ever to get back into a relationship with the kind of person you are. A.

But who could he send it to? Who could be his go-between?

It was talking about Christmas with Winston that brought him what could be a solution. Helen had told him of friends in Gloucester with whom she and her mother and, since her marriage, Roger as well, spent every Christmas. He had never heard their address and their name eluded him, though Helen had mentioned it. She had told him, he remembered, that it was Latin for a priest . . .

"Linthea and I," Winston said, "will still be on our honeymoon. Lovely having Christmas in Jamaica, only I feel a bit bad about Leroy. Maybe we ought to take him. On our *honeymoon?* Perhaps I'm being too conventional, perhaps . . ."

"What's the Latin for a priest?" said Anthony abruptly.

Winston stared at him. "Sorry if I'm boring you."

"You're not boring me. I hope you'll have a fabulous honeymoon. I should be so lucky. Take the whole Merton Street Primary School with you if you like, but just tell me the Latin for a priest."

"*Pontifex, pontificis,* masculine."

He knew it was the right name as soon as he heard it. Pontifex. He'd go to the public library, the main branch in the High Street, where they kept telephone directories for the whole country. "Thanks," he said.

"You're welcome," said Winston. "Just a dictionary, I am. Mr. Liddell or Mr. Scott."

There were three Pontifexes (or *pontifices,* as Winston would have put it) in the city of Gloucester. But A.W. at 26 Dittisham Road was obviously the one, Miss Margaret and Sir F. being unlikely candidates. Anthony prepared an envelope: Mrs. Pontifex, 26 Dittisham Road, Gloucester, and on the flap: Sender, A. Johnson, 2/142 Trinity Road, London W15 6HD. The letter to Helen went into a blank, smaller envelope to be inserted inside it. But there would have to be a covering letter.

Anthony knew he couldn't write to a woman he had never met, instructing her to pass an enclosure to another woman without the knowledge of that woman's husband. But that wouldn't be necessary. Helen and Roger would arrive at the Pontifex home on, say, Christmas Eve. Mrs. Pontifex would hand his letter over to Helen either when they were alone together—perhaps in Mrs. Pontifex's bedroom immediately after their arrival—or else, and more likely, in public and full view of a company of festive relatives. Did that matter? Anthony thought not. This way, even if Roger were to demand to see it, Helen would see it first.

Dear Mrs. Pontifex, I know that Mrs. Garvist will be spending Christmas with you and I wonder if you would be kind enough to give her the enclosed when you see her. I have mislaid her present address, otherwise I would not trouble you. Yours sincerely, Anthony Johnson.

It looked, he thought, peculiar, to say the least. He had mislaid the address of someone with the rare name of Garvist whom he obviously knew well, but was in possession of the address of someone with the equally rare name of Pontifex whom he didn't know at all. If one name could be found in the phone book so could the other. He stuck a stamp on the envelope. He looked at this result of so much complicated effort. Was it worth it? Would any possible outcome mitigate the depression which enclosed him? The letter need not, in any case, be sent till a few days before Christmas. Pushing it to one side with a heap of books and papers and notes, he wondered if, in the end, he would send it at all.

~~~~~~~~

When Arthur spoke of "my solicitor" he meant a firm in Kenbourne Lane which had acted for him twenty years before in the matter of proving Auntie Gracie's meagre will. Since then he had never communicated with this firm or been inside its offices, but he went there now and it cost him fifteen pounds to be told that unless there were any repairs outstanding to the fabric of his flat, he hadn't a leg to stand on against Stanley Caspian in the matter of the rent increase. Although, as he put it to himself exaggeratedly, the rest of the place was falling down, Flat 2 was in fact in good order. Almost wishing that the roof would spring a leak, Arthur managed some petty revenge by telling a young couple whom he found waiting in the hall before Stanley Caspian's Saturday arrival that Flat 1 had macabre associations and that its rent could be knocked down to eight pounds a week by anyone who cared to try it on. The young couple argued with Stanley but they didn't take the Kotowskys' flat.

The police had not reappeared. Everyone took it for granted Brian Kotowsky had murdered his wife. But Arthur remembered the case of John Reginald Halliday Christie. Christie had murdered, among others, another man's wife and that man had been hanged for it. But in the end that murder had been brought home to the true perpetrator. Arthur never relaxed his surveillance of the post or failed to put his door on the latch when he heard anyone use the telephone. Wednesday, November 27, had been a bad evening but it had passed without Anthony Johnson making a call. No letters from Bristol had come for more than a fortnight. Surely there would be none? Arthur observed Anthony Johnson coming and going at his irregular hours, a little dejected, perhaps, as if some of that youthful glow and vigour which he had noticed on their first meeting, had gone out of him. But we all have to grow up and face, Arthur thought, the reality and earnestness of life. Once, passing beneath his window, Anthony Johnson raised a hand and waved to him. It wasn't a particularly enthusiastic wave, but Arthur would have distrusted it if it had been. It signified to him only that Anthony Johnson bore him no malice.

On the morning of Saturday, December 7, he wrote a stiff letter to his solicitor, deprecating the high cost of such negative advice but nevertheless enclosing a cheque for fifteen pounds. He always paid his bills promptly, having an undefined fear of nemesis descending should he be in debt to anyone for more than a day or two. At nine he saw the postman cross the street and he went down to take in the mail. Nothing but a rates demand for Stanley Caspian which shouldn't, by rights, have come to Trinity Road at all.

Li-li Chan's rent envelope was on the hall table and so was Winston Mervyn's. Anthony Johnson's, however, was missing. Arthur listened warily outside the door of Room 2. Silence, then the clink of a tea cup against a saucer. He knocked softly on the door and gave his apologetic cough.

"Yes?"

"It's Mr. Johnson, Mr. Johnson," said Arthur, feeling this was ridiculous, but not knowing how else to put it.

"One minute."

About a quarter of a minute passed and then the door was opened by Anthony Johnson in jeans and a sweater which had obviously been pulled on in haste. The room was freezing, the electric fire having perhaps only just been switched on. From the state of the bed and the presence on the bedside table of a half-consumed cup of tea, it was evident that Anthony Johnson had been having a lie-in. And to his caller's extreme disapproval, he intended to resume it, for, having offered Arthur a cup of tea which was refused, he got back into bed fully clothed.

"I hope you'll excuse the intrusion, but it's about the little matter of the rent."

"You needn't have bothered. I'd have put it out before Caspian came." Anthony Johnson finished his tea. "It's on the table," he said casually, "among all that other stuff."

"All that other stuff" was a formidable array (or muddle, as Arthur put it to himself) of books, some closed, some open and face downwards, scattered sheets of foolscap, dog-eared notebooks and a partially completed manuscript.

"With your permission," Arthur said, and delicately picked about in the mess as if it were a pile of noxious garbage. He came upon the brown rent envelope under a weighty tome entitled *Human Behaviour and Social Processes*.

"The rent book and my cheque are in there."

Arthur said nothing. Under the rent envelope was another, stamped and addressed, but without his glasses he was unable, from this distance, to read the address. At once it occurred to him that this letter might be to H in Bristol. He thought quickly, said almost as quickly:

"I have to go to the post with a letter of my own. Would you care for me to take this one of yours?"

Anthony Johnson's hesitation was unmistakeable. Was he remembering that other occasion on which Arthur had posted a letter for him and the unfortunate antagonism that action had led to? Or did he perhaps suspect a tampering with his post? Anthony Johnson threw back the bed covers, got up and came over to the table. He picked up the envelope and looked at it in silence, indecisively, deep in thought. Arthur managed a considerate patient smile, but inwardly he was trembling. It must be to her, it must be. Why else would the man linger over it like this, wondering, no doubt, whether posting it would risk a violent confrontation with the woman's husband.

At last Anthony Johnson looked up. He handed the letter to

Arthur with a funny swift gesture as if he must either be rid of it quickly or not at all.

"O.K.," he said. "Thanks."

Once more in the hall and alone, Arthur held the envelope up to within two inches of his eyes. Then he put on his glasses to make absolutely sure. But it was all right. The letter was addressed to a Mrs. Pontifex in Gloucester. He was savouring his relief when Stanley Caspian banged in, sucking a toffee. Arthur put the kettle on without waiting to be asked and handed Stanley his rents. Stanley opened Winston Mervyn's envelope first.

"Well, my God, if Mervyn's not going now! Given in his poxy notice for the first week of Jan."

"A little bird told me he's getting married."

Stanley munched ill-temperedly, jabbing so hard into Arthur's rent book that his pen made a hole in the page. "That'll be the whole of the first floor vacant. Makes you wonder what the world's coming to."

"The rats," said Arthur, "might be said to be leaving the sinking ship."

"Not you, though, eh? Oh no. Those as have unfurnished tenancies don't go till they're carried out feet first. You'll die here, me old Arthur."

"I'm sure I hope so," said Arthur. "Now, if I could have my little envelope?"

He took it and set off with his laundry, pausing outside Kemal's Kebab House to drop both letters in the pillar box.

19

During the week which followed Arthur was oppressively aware of the emptiness of 142 Trinity Road. Li-li had never been at home much, was flying to Taiwan for Christmas, and now Winston Mervyn was out every night. Soon he too would be gone. Then, if the pressure of the London housing shortage wasn't strong enough to overcome people's semi-superstitious distaste for 142, he and Anthony Johnson would in effect be the sole tenants. He would once have welcomed the idea. Once he had savoured those moments when he had had the house to himself, when the last of them to leave in the mornings had given the front door a final bang. And he had dreamed of being its only occupant, living high on the crest of silent emptiness, while she who inhabited the depths below awaited the attentions and whims of her master.

But now that empty silence disturbed him. For three nights out of the seven no light fell on to the court from the window of Room 2, and the dark well he could see below him when he drew his curtains brought him temptations he had no way of yielding to. It frightened him even to think of them, but these suppressed thoughts blossomed in dreams like tubers which, put away in the dark, throw out sickly, sluglike shoots. Not since he was a young man had he dreamed of that act he had three times performed. But he dreamed of it now and awoke one morning hanging half out of bed, his hands clenched as if in spasm round the leg of his bedside table which, unknowingly, he had dragged towards him.

The postman had ceased to call. In all the years Arthur had

been there no such week as this, without a single letter, had passed. It was as if the Post Office were on strike. Of course it was easily explicable. Winston Mervyn had seldom received any post except that from estate agents; Li-li's father wouldn't write when he expected to see his daughter next week; little had ever come for Anthony Johnson but those mauve-grey Bristol envelopes. And yet this also seemed to contribute to Arthur's feeling that all the forces of life were withdrawing from the house and leaving it as a kind of mausoleum for himself.

But on the morning of Saturday, December 14, something resembling a convulsion took place in it, like a death throe. The phone ringing wakened him. It rang for Winston Mervyn three times before nine o'clock. Then he heard Winston Mervyn running up and down the stairs, Anthony Johnson in Mervyn's room, Anthony Johnson and Mervyn talking, laughing. He went down to see if there was, by chance, any post. There wasn't. The door of Room 1 was open, music playing above the whine of the vacuum cleaner. Li-li had decided, unseasonably and uniquely, to spring-clean her room. And Stanley Caspian, usually so mindful of the fabric of his property, added to the noise by slamming the front door so hard that plaster specks lay scattered on his car coat like dandruff.

Stanley detained him so long with moans about the rates, the cruelty of the government towards honest landlords, and the fastidiousness of prospective tenants that he was late in getting to the shops. Every machine at the launderette was taken. He had to leave his washing in the care of Mr. Grainger's nephew's wife who was distant with him and demanded an extra twenty pence for service.

"I never heard of such a thing," said Arthur.

"Take it or leave it. There's inflation for me same as for others."

Arthur would have liked to say more but he was afraid it might get back to Mr. Grainger, so he contented himself with a severe, "I'll call back for it at two sharp."

"Four'd be more like," said the woman, "what with this rush," and she paid Arthur no compliments as to the superiority of his linen.

It was a June-skied day but hazeless and clearer than any June day could be, and the sunlight was made icy by a razor wind. Angrily, Arthur shouted at the children who were climbing on the statues. They took no notice beyond shouting back at him a word which, though familiar to any resident of West Kenbourne, still brought a blush to his face.

A taxi stood outside 142, and as he approached, Winston Mervyn and Anthony Johnson came out of the house and went up to it. Arthur thought how awkward and embarrassed he would feel if called upon to say to a taxi driver what Winston Mervyn now said:

"Kenbourne Register Office, please."

He said it in a bold, loud voice, as if he were proud of himself, and favoured everyone with a broad smile. Arthur would have liked to pass on up the steps without a word, but he knew better than to neglect his social obligations, particularly as Stanley Caspian had told him this coloured fellow, obviously well off, was buying a house in North Kenbourne.

"Let me offer you my best wishes for your future happiness, Mr. Mervyn," he said.

"Thanks very much."

"A fine day for your wedding," said Arthur, "though somewhat chilly."

He went indoors and passed Li-li going out, her rare effort at cleaning finished or abandoned. Again he was alone. He cooked his lunch, scoured the flat, watched Michael Redgrave in *The Captive Heart* on television. It wasn't till darkness began to close in and lights came on in the tall houses opposite that he remembered he still had to collect his washing.

~~~~~~~~~

Winston had engaged one of the dining rooms at the Grand Duke for his wedding reception, and there at one-thirty the bride and groom, Leroy, Anthony, Winston's brother and sister-in-law, and Linthea's sister and brother-in-law sat down to lunch. Linthea gave Anthony a rose from the bouquet she was carrying.

"There, that means you'll be the next to marry."

He felt a painful squeeze of the heart. But he smiled down at the beautiful girl in her apple-green silk dress and said, "That's only for bridesmaids."

"For best men too. It's an old West Indian custom."

Cries of denial, gales of laughter greeted this. Anthony made a speech which he felt was feeble, though it was received with applause. He could hardly bear to look at Winston and Linthea, whose exchanged glances and secret decorous smiles spoke of happiness enjoyed and anticipated.

At four they all went back to Brasenose Avenue to collect Linthea's luggage and then to Trinity Road for Winston's. From the call box on the landing Winston phoned London Airport to check his honeymoon flight to Jamaica and was told it had been delayed three hours. By this time Leroy had already been carried off by his aunt, with whom he was to stay, and Linthea felt a dislike of going back to the empty flat. At a loose end, they were debating how they should kill the intervening time, when the front door, which had been left on the latch, crashed heavily, and a voice called up the stairs:

"The wedding guest, he beat his breast!"

Jonathan Dean.

"Thought I'd try and catch you before you left, old man. Wish you Godspeed and all that." He showed, Anthony thought, no scars from grief over his dead friend, but seemed stouter and ruddier. Half-way up the stairs he met them coming down. "Did I hear someone mention killing time? How about a quick one or a few slow ones up the Lily?"

"It's not five," said Winston.

Jonathan agreed but said it wanted only ten minutes and that tempus was fugiting as usual. At this point Li-li emerged from Room 1 to be met by a look of frank lechery from Jonathan, who made a joke with heavy play on her name and that of the pub which evoked screams of merriment from Winston's sister-in-law. And so, without much show of enthusiasm on the part of either bride or groom, the whole party, now swelled to seven, made their way towards the Waterlily.

When they reached the corner of Magdalen Hill and Balliol Street—by common unspoken consent, they avoided Oriel Mews —Anthony saw, standing on the other side of the street, waiting for the lights to change, a familiar lean figure in silver-grey overcoat and carrying an orange plastic laundry bag. The man's face had the sore, reddish look he had noticed before, and there was something prickly and resentful in his whole bearing as if he took the persistent greenness of the traffic light and the stream of vehicles as an affront aimed personally at him. In that crowd, London working class, hippy-costumed drop-outs, brown immigrants, his clothes and his air set him apart and enclosed him in loneliness. Time and change had passed him by. He was a sad and bitter anachronism.

Anthony touched Winston's arm. "Should we ask old Johnson to join us for a drink? It's up to you, it's your party, but it seems a bit cold not to . . ."

Before he could finish, Winston had hailed Arthur Johnson who had begun to cross the road. "I'm glad you saw him," he said to Anthony. "He was rather nice to me this morning with his good wishes, and seeing everyone else in the house is here, it's the least we can do. Mr. Johnson!" he called. "Can you spare a few minutes to come and celebrate with us in the Waterlily?"

Anthony wasn't surprised to see that Arthur Johnson was flummoxed, even shocked, by the suggestion. First came the mottled flush, then a stream of excuses. "I couldn't possibly—most kind but out of the question—a busy evening ahead of me—you must count me out, you really must, Mr. Mervyn."

It seemed definite enough. But Anthony—and evidently Arthur Johnson—had reckoned without West Indian hospitality and West Indian enthusiastic pressure. In argument, Arthur Johnson would perhaps have won, but he was given no chance to argue, the situation being managed by Winston's brother, a man of overpowering bonhomie. And Anthony who in the past had been irritated by and sorry for Arthur Johnson, now felt neither anger nor pity. It was all he could do to stop himself laughing aloud at the sight of this finicky and austere-looking man propelled into the saloon bar of the Waterlily between Perry Mervyn and Jonathan Dean. Arthur Johnson looked amazed and frightened. Still clutching his carrier bag, he had the air of some gentleman burglar of fiction apprehended by plainclothes policemen, the bag, of course, containing the spoils of crime. And now it was Li-li who took the bag from him, ignoring his protests and thrusting it under the settle on which she and Jonathan sat down with their victim between them.

~~~~~~~~~~~

It was a violation, a kidnapping almost, Arthur thought, too affronted to speak. He had never before entered the Waterlily which, in his youth, had been pointed out to him by Auntie Gracie as a den of iniquity. Bewildered, crushed by shyness, he sat stiff and silent while Jonathan Dean paid Li-li compliments across him and Li-li giggled in return. The stout and very black woman who faced him added to his discomfiture by asking him in rapid succession what he did for a living, if he was married and how long had he lived in Trinity Road. He was saved from answering her fourth question—didn't he think her new sister-in-law absolutely lovely?—by Anthony Johnson's asking him what he would drink. Arthur replied, inevitably, that he would have a small brandy.

"Claret is the liquor for boys, port for men, but he who aspires to be a hero must drink brandy." Having quoted this, Dean roared with laughter and said it was by Dr. Johnson.

Arthur didn't know what he meant but felt he was getting at him personally and perhaps also at Anthony Johnson. He wondered how soon he could make his escape. The brandy came and with it a variety of longer, less strong, drinks for the others, which made Arthur wonder if he had made a too expensive choice or even committed some gross social error. Two entirely separate conversations began to be conducted round the table, one between Li-li, Dean, and Mervyn's sister-in-law, the other between the bridal couple and Mervyn's brother. And Arthur was aware of the isolation of himself and the "other" Johnson, both of whom were left out of these exchanges. Anthony Johnson looked rather ill—had drunk too much, Arthur supposed, at whatever carousing had been going on since lunchtime—and he began turning over in his mind various opening gambits for a conversation between them. As the only English people present, for the loathsome Dean didn't count and was very likely an Irishman, anyway, it was their duty to present some sort of solid front. And he had opened his mouth to speak of the severe frost which the television had forecast for that night, when Dean, raising his glass in what he called a nuptial toast, launched into a speech.

For some moments this was listened to in silence, though Winston Mervyn seemed fidgety. Didn't like someone else stealing his thunder, Arthur thought. And Dean was certainly airing his education, spouting streams of stuff which couldn't have been thought up on the spur of the moment but must have been written down first. It was all about love and marriage, and Arthur actually chuckled when Dean levelled his gaze on Mervyn's stout brother-in-law and said that in marriage a man becomes slack and selfish and undergoes a fatty degeneration of his moral being. At the same time he was aware that under the table a heavily shod foot was groping across his ankles to find a daintily shod foot. He drew in his knees.

"To marry," said Dean, "is to domesticate the Recording Angel. Once you are married there is nothing left for you, not even suicide, but to be good."

Only Li-li laughed. The Mervyn relatives looked blank. Winston Mervyn got up abruptly and stalked to the bar, while Anthony Johnson, with a violence which alarmed Arthur because he couldn't at all understand it, said:

"For God's sake, shut up! D'you ever stop and think what you're saying?"

Dean's face fell. He blushed. But he leaned across Arthur almost as if he wasn't there and whispered on beery breath into Li-li's face, "You like me, don't you, darling? You're not so bloody fastidious."

Li-li giggled. There was some awkward dodging about, and then Arthur realised she was kissing Dean behind his back.

"Perhaps," he said, "you'd care to change places with me?"

Why this should have caused so much mirth—general laughter after awkwardness—he was unable to understand, but he thought he could take it as his chance to leave. And he would have left had not Mervyn returned at that moment with another tray of drinks including a second small brandy. He edged along the settle, leaving Li-li and Dean huddled together.

It was a pity, in a way, about the brandy, because it necessarily brought memories and associations. But without it he couldn't have borne the party at all, couldn't even have looked on the conviviality or withstood the incomprehensible warring tensions. Now, however, when he had drunk the last vapourous, fiery drop of it, he jumped to his feet and said rather shrilly that he must go. He must no longer trespass on their hospitality, he must leave.

"Stand not upon the order of your going, but go at once," said Dean.

Such rudeness, even if it came out of a book, wasn't to be borne. Arthur made a stiff little bow in the direction of Mervyn and the new Mrs. Mervyn, gave a stiff little nod of the head in exchange for their farewells, and escaped.

The joy of getting out was heady. He hurried home through the mews, that dark throat where once, in its jaws, he had made death swallow a woman who flitted like a great black bird. A mouse, a baby, Maureen Cowan, Bridget O'Neill, Vesta Kotowsky . . . But, no. Home now, encountering no one.

At the top of the empty house he settled down to watch John Wayne discharging yet again the duties of a United States cavalry colonel. He leaned against the brown satin cushion, cool, clean, luxurious. The film ended at half-past eight. Rather late to begin on his ironing, but better late than on Sunday. For twenty years he had done his ironing on a Saturday.

Entering the kitchen to get out the ironing board and the folded linen, he looked in vain for the orange plastic bag. It wasn't there. He had left it behind in the Waterlily.

20

The first to leave the party was Jonathan Dean. Anthony, aware that for the past half-hour Jonathan had been busy entangling his legs with Li-li's under the table, supposed they would remain after he and the Mervyns had gone and that the evening would end for them by Li-li's becoming Vesta's successor. Things happened differently. Li-li departed to the passageway that housed the ladies' lavatory. It also housed a phone, and when she came back she announced that she must soon go, as she had a date at seven-thirty. Junia Mervyn, a woman who seemed to take delight in the general discomfiture of men, laughed merrily.

"What about me?" said Jonathan truculently.

Li-li giggled. "You like to come too? Wait and I go call my friend again."

"You know very well I didn't mean that."

"Me, I don't know what men mean. I don't try to know. I love them all a little bit. You like to go on my list? Then when I come back from Taiwan I make you number three, four?" She and Junia clutched each other, laughing. Jonathan got up and without a backward look or a word to his hosts, banged out of the pub.

The men were heavily, awkwardly, silent. Anthony, suddenly and not very aptly identifying, felt through his depression a surge of angry misogyny. And he said before he could stop himself:

"As a connoisseur of bad behaviour in women, I'd give you my prize."

Li-li pouted. She sidled up to him, opening her eyes wide, trying her wiles. He wondered afterwards if he would actually have struck her, at least have given her a savage push, had Winston not interrupted by announcing it was time to leave for the airport.

He interposed his body, spoke smoothly. "Feel like coming with us, Anthony? My brother will give you a lift back."

Anthony said he would. In a low voice he apologised to Linthea. She kissed his cheek.

"Have women really behaved so badly to you?"

"One has. It doesn't matter. Forget it, Linthea, please."

"I'm not to bother my pretty little head about it?"

Anthony smiled. This description of her head, goddesslike with its crown of coiled braids, was so inept that he was about to correct her with a compliment when Winston's brother said:

"Your friend left his shopping behind."

"He's not our fliend," said Li-li, "and it's not shopping, it's washing." She pulled it out from under the settle, pointing to and giggling at the topmost item it contained, a pair of underpants. "You," she said imperiously to Anthony, "take it back for him."

"Suppose you do that? I'm going to the airport."

"Me take nasty old man's washing out on my date?"

"You've got time to take it home first," said Winston. "It's only a quarter past seven." Always a controller of situations, he closed her little white hand round the handles of the orange plastic bag and placed her firmly but gently back on the settle. A fresh glass of martini in front of her, she sat silenced, looking very small and young. "That's a good girl," said Winston.

The night was cruelly cold, its clarity turning all the lights to sharply cut gems. Linthea took Winston's arm and shivered against him as if, now she was going home, she could allow herself to feel the cold of an English winter for the first time. As they crossed the street, Anthony saw a familiar red sports car draw up outside the Waterlily.

~~~~~~~~~

The contents of the bag were worth, Arthur calculated, about fifty pounds—all his working shirts, his underwear, bed linen . . .

It was unthinkable to leave them in that rough public house which would fill up, on a Saturday night, with God knew what riff-raff. But to go out at this hour into darkness?

One of them might, just might, have brought the bag back for him. He went out on to the landing, and the light from his own hall shed a little radiance as far as the top of the stairs. But below was a pit of blackness. There was nothing outside his door, nothing at the head of the stairs. He put on lights, descended. First he knocked on Li-li's door, then on that of Room 2. But he knew it was in vain. Slits of light always showed round the doors when the occupants of the rooms were in.

If only he dared forget about it, leave it till the Waterlily opened in the morning. But, no, he couldn't risk losing so much valuable property. And it was only a step to the pub, less than five minutes' walk. He went back upstairs and put on his overcoat.

He walked rapidly up Camera Street, keeping his eyes lowered. But Balliol Street was full of people, corpses in brown grave clothes, their faces and their dress turned pallid or khaki by the colour-excluding sodium lamps. Yellow-brown too was the sports car parked outside Kemal's Kebab House, but Arthur recognized it as belonging to one of Li-li's young men. Only the traffic lights were bright enough to compete with that yellow glare. Their green and scarlet hurt his eyes and made him blink.

Entering the Waterlily on his own recalled to him those three previous occasions on which he had gone into a public house alone. He pushed away the memory, reminding himself how near he was to Trinity Road. The pub was crowded now and Arthur had to queue. He asked for a small brandy, though he hadn't meant to buy a drink at all. But he needed the warmth and the comfort of it to combat the agonies of embarrassment he passed through while the licencee asked the barman and the barman asked the barmaid—in bellowing amused voices—for a Mr. Johnson's laundry bag.

"You were with those people who'd got married, weren't you?" Arthur nodded.

"An orange-coloured bag? That Chinese girl took it. I saw her go out of the door with it."

He gave a gasp of relief. Li-li was in Kemal's, and his laundry, no doubt, was in that very car he had walked past. He almost ran out of the Waterlily. He crossed the mews entrance. There were so many cars lining the street and all their paintbox colours reduced to tones of sepia. But the sports car wasn't among them. Li-li and her escort had gone.

Arthur stood shaking outside the restaurant, and the hot, spicy smell that wafted to him from its briefly opened door brought a gust of nausea in which he could taste the stinging warmth of brandy. And for support he rested one arm along the convex frosted top of the pillar box. All he wanted, he told himself, was to get his washing, secure it from those who, with reasonless malice, had taken it and were keeping it from him.

Where did people go when they went out in the evening? To pubs, restaurants, cinemas. Li-li had already been to a pub, a restaurant. Arthur considered, his head beginning to drum. Then he crossed the road in the direction of Magdalen Hill and the Taj Mahal.

Now the whole corner was boarded up, the waste ground as well as the area where the demolished houses had been, where Auntie Gracie's house had been. It was fenced in blankly with a row of those old doors builders save and use for this purpose. As Arthur passed close by he could see through the yellow glare that each was painted in some pale bathroom shade, pink, green, cream. Closed, nailed together, they seemed to shut off great epochs of his life. He went past Grainger's and the station. A train running under the street made strong vibrations run up through his body.

The film showing at the Taj Mahal wasn't truly Indian but something from farther east. The slant-eyed faces, the heads crowned with jewelled, pagoda-shaped headdresses on the poster outside told him that. And this gave force to his feeling that it was here Li-li had come. But there was no parking space in Kenbourne Lane with its double yellow band coursing the edge of the pavement. Suppose she was inside? He wouldn't be able to find her or fetch her out. Still he lingered at the foot of the steps, looking almost wistfully in at the foyer, so much the same as ever yet so dreadfully changed. Hundreds of times he had passed through those swing doors with Auntie Gracie, but it was more than twenty years since he had visited any cinema except that which his own living room afforded.

He wouldn't go in there now. Behind the cinema was a vast council car park. He would go into that car park and find the red sports car. It was unlikely to be locked, for the young were all feckless and indifferent to the value of property. He made his way down the path between shops and cinema, hearing the oriental music which reached him through the tall, cream-painted ramparts of the Taj Mahal. It made a huge, pale cliff, overshadowing the car park, which was unlit, though semi-circled at its perimeter with many of those yellow lights and with silvery white ones as well. There was no one in the attendant's hut at the entrance, there was no one anywhere. Arthur passed beside the barrier, the sword-shaped arm that would rise to allow the passage of a vehicle.

Cars stood in long regular rows. Underfoot it wasn't tarmac or concrete but a gravelly mud, beginning now to freeze into hardness. He could walk on it with soundless footfalls. Slowly he crept along, scanning car after car, pausing sometimes to stare along the lines of car roofs that gleamed dully like aquatic beasts slumbering side by side on some northern moonlit coast. But it was a false moonlight, the heavy purple sky suffused only by street lamps.

When he reached the southernmost point of the great irregular quadrangle, a sense of the absurdity of what he was doing began gradually to penetrate his brandy haze. He wasn't going to find the sports car, or if he did he wouldn't dare to touch it. He had no evidence that Li-li had ever passed this way or entered the Taj Mahal. Not for this purpose had he come into the solitary half-dark of this place. He had come for the reason he always ventured into the dark and the loneliness. . . .

But there were no women here. None of those creatures who threatened his liberty, were always a danger to him, were here. And he could only find one of them if he left the car park by the narrow gate behind him, impassable to vehicles, that led to a path into Brasenose Avenue. With painful lust he envisioned that little defile, but he turned his back on it, turned from its direction, and forced his legs to push him back towards the hut between the ranks of cars.

Then, as he emerged into a wider aisle, he saw that he was no longer alone. A car, one of those tinny, perched-up little Citroëns, had nosed in and was searching for a space. Arthur drew himself up, narrowing and trimming his body so as to present a respectable and decorous air. Almost greater than that growing, not-to-be-permitted desire was the need to appear to any watcher as a law-abiding car owner with legitimate business here. The Citroën dived into a well of darkness between two larger cars. Arthur was only a dozen yards away from it. He saw the driver get out, and the driver was a woman.

~~~~~~~~~

A young girl, tallish and very slender, wearing jeans and an Afghan coat with furry edges and embroidery which gleamed a little in the light from pale distant lamps. Her hair was a golden aureole, a mass of metallic-looking filaments that hung below her shoulders. The car door open, she was bending over the interior, adjusting to the steering column some thiefproof locking device. He saw her high-heeled boots, the leather wrinkling over thin ankles, and he felt a constriction in his throat. He could taste brandied bile.

Now, soft-footed, he was a yard behind her. The girl straightened and closed the car door. But it refused to catch. She pulled it wide and shut it with a hard slam. The noise made a vast explosion in Arthur's ears as he raised his hands and leapt upon her from behind, digging his fingers into her neck.

The earth rocked as he held onto that surprisingly strong and sinewy neck, and the huge purple sky blazed at him, burning his eyes. The girl was resisting, strong as he, stronger. . . . She gave a powerful twist and her elbow thrust back hard into his diaphragm. He staggered at the sudden pain, slackening his hold, and a fist swung into his face, hard bone against his teeth. With a strangled grunt he fell back against the next car, sliding down its slippery bodywork. Her face loomed over his, contorted, savage, and Arthur let out a cry, for it was the face of a young man with a hooked nose, stubble on his upper lip, and a cape of coarse hair streaming. The fist swung again, this time to his eye. Arthur slid down onto the frozen mud and lay there, half under the oil-blackened chassis of the other car.

He didn't move, although he was conscious. A hand turned

him over, a sharp-toed boot kicked his ribs. He made no sound, but lay there with his eyes closed. The boy was standing over him, breathing heavily, making sucking sounds of satisfaction and triumph. Then he heard footsteps pounding away towards the hut and the barrier and there was a terrible deep silence.

Arthur hauled himself up, clinging to the wings of both cars. His face was wet with blood running from his upper lip and his head was banging as it had never banged from desire. He forced his eyes into focus so that he could see the shining, sleeping cars, the glittering, frosted ground. No attendant coming, no one. He crawled between the cars, clutching here at a wing mirror, there at a door handle, until at last the strength that comes from terror brought him to an upright stance. He staggered. The icy air, unimpeded, was like a further blow to his face. He tasted the salt blood trickling between his teeth.

Still the hut was empty, the path between cinema and shops deserted. Covering his face with the clean white handkerchief he always carried, he made himself walk down that path, walk slowly, although he wanted to run and scream. Kenbourne Lane. No crowd was gathered, no huddle of passers-by stood staring in the direction taken by a running boy with golden hair. No one looked at Arthur. It was the season for colds, for muffled faces. He went on past the station until he came to Grainger's gates. Thank God they weren't padlocked but closed with a Yale lock. Holding up the handkerchief, he unlocked the gates, the conscientious surveyor who works Saturday nights despite a cold in the head. They closed behind him and he sank heavily against them.

But he must reach his own office. There, for a while, he would be safe. The little house of glass and cedarwood was an island and a haven in the big bare yard. He crawled to it because his legs, which had carried him so well when their strength had most been needed, had buckled now and were half-paralysed. From the ground, slippery with frost, he reached up and unlocked the door.

It was cold inside, colder than in the open air. The Adler stood on the desk, shrouded in its cover; the wastepaper basket was empty; the place smelt faintly of bubble gum. Arthur collapsed on to the floor and lay there, his body shaking with gasping sobs. He staunched the blood, which might otherwise have got onto the carpet, first with his handkerchief, then with his scarf. As the handkerchief became unusable, black with blood, he heard the wail of sirens, distant and keening at first, then screaming on an ear-splitting rise and fall as the police cars came over the lights into Magdalen Hill.

21

West Kenbourne was populated with police. It seemed to Anthony, returning from the airport in Perry Mervyn's car, that every other pedestrian in Balliol Street was a policeman. Since they had turned from the High Street up Kenbourne Lane, he had counted five police cars.

"Maybe someone robbed a bank," said Junia.

It was half-past eleven, but lights were still on in the Dalmatian and the Waterlily and their doors stood open. Police were in the pubs and standing in the doorways, questioning customers as they left. From behind the improvised fence that shut off the waste ground, the beams from policemen's torches cut the air in long pale swaying shafts.

"Must have been a bank," said Perry, and he and his wife offered sage opinions—they were in perfect agreement—as to the comparative innocuousness of bank robbery. It could hardly be called morally wrong, it harmed no one, and so on. Anthony, though grateful for the lift, wasn't sorry when they arrived at 142 Trinity Road.

He thanked them and they exchanged undertakings not to lose touch. Anthony supposed, and supposed they supposed, that they would never meet again. Waving, he watched the car depart, its occupants having declared they would drive around for a while and try to find out what was going on.

Nothing was going on in Trinity Road. A hundred and forty-two was in total darkness. He went indoors and walked slowly along the passage towards Room 2. The police hunt afforded him no interest, brought him no curiosity. Nothing was able to divert

him from the all-enclosing grey misery which had succeeded disbelief, anger, pain. The wedding, the happiness of Winston and
Linthea, had served only to vary his depression with fresh pain.
And in the airport lounge, where they had sat drinking coffee, a
horrible aspect of that pain had shown itself. For that busy
place, with its continual comings and goings, was peopled for
him with Helens, with versions of Helen. Every fair head, turned
from him, might turn again and show him her face. One girl,
from a distance, had her walk; another, talking animatedly to a
man who might be Roger—how would he know?—moved her
hands in Helen gestures, and her laugh, soft and clear, reached
him as Helen's laugh. Once he was certain. He even got to his
feet, staring, catching his breath. The others must have thought
him crazy, hallucinated.

He put his key into the door lock. But before he could enter
Room 2 the front door opened and Li-li came in, carrying Arthur
Johnson's washing bag.

"Have you been carting that round all night?" said Anthony
disagreeably.

"Is not all night. Is only twelve." She waved the bag at him.
"There, you shall take it to him now. He will be so pleased to
have it safe."

"Knowing him, I should think he's nearly gone out of his mind
worrying about it. And you can take it to him yourself."

But, as Li-li with a pout and a giggle disappeared round the
first bend of the stairs, Anthony thought he had better follow
her. He caught up with her as she was mounting the second
flight.

"He'll be asleep. He always goes to bed early. Leave it outside
his door."

"O.K." Li-li dropped the bag on the landing. "Nasty, nasty, to
be old and go to bed at midnight." She gave Anthony a sweet
provocative smile. "You like some Chinese tea?"

"No, thanks. I go to bed at midnight too." He walked into
Room 2 and closed the door firmly. It was some time before he
fell asleep, for Li-li, preparing for her journey on the following
day, revenged herself by packing noisily, banging her wardrobe
door and apparently throwing shoes across the room, until after
three.

Arthur heard the police get Grainger's doors open half an hour after he had hidden himself in the office. He saw the beams of their torches searchlighting the yard. They came up to the office and walked round it, but because the door hadn't been forced and no window was broken, they went away. He heard the gates clang behind them.

His lip had stopped bleeding. When it was safe to get up from the floor, he wrapped his handkerchief in a sheet of flimsy paper and thrust it into his coat pocket. Very little light was available to him, only a distant sheen from the lamps of Magdalen Hill. He didn't dare put the light on or even the electric fire, though it was bitterly cold. His scarf was patched and streaked with blood, but not so badly stained that he couldn't wear it. It was of the utmost importance to leave no blood on the haircord or as fingerprints. But the yellow twilight was sufficient to show him that the haircord was unmarked. He licked his fingers till they were free of the salty taste.

Then he lay down again on the floor, sleepless, letting the long slow hours pass. His ribs ached on the left side but he didn't think the kick had broken a bone. Outside they would comb the whole area. When they couldn't find him they would leave the area and look further afield. Perhaps they wouldn't come to Trinity Road at all.

Would it never get light? Light would show any passer-by his injured face—if only he had the means to see how injured it was! —but a man walking solitary in the dark small hours would attract more attention. When the yellowness retreated into the milky grey of dawn, he dragged himself to his feet and looked out of the window on to the deserted yard. His body was stiff, every limb aching, and a sharp, fluctuating pain teased his left side.

His watch had broken in the fall and the hands still showed twenty past nine. It must now be about eleven hours later than that. His watch had broken but not his glasses, which remained intact in their case. He put them on, although they were reading glasses that threw the world out of focus, but they would help disguise his eye. As to his lip—he licked a corner of his scarf and worked blindly at the cut, wincing because the rough fibres prickled the edges of the wound. But the morning was very cold and now he saw that a thin sleet had begun to fall, little granules of ice that melted as they struck the ground. The kind of day, he thought, when a man with a muffled face is accepted as normal.

Shaking a little, controlling his shaking as best he could, he went out of the office, locking the door behind him. He had left no vestige of his presence. As he approached the gates, the falling sleet thickened into a storm. Snow, the first of the year, swirled about him, flakes of it stinging his lip. He pulled the scarf up to cover his mouth and, with lowered head, took what was a kind of plunge into Magdalen Hill.

There was no one about but a boy delivering Sunday papers. His encounter with the girl-boy in the car park had happened too late at night for there to be anything about it in the papers, and this little boy in thick coat and balaclava didn't look at him. A man walking a retriever in Balliol Street didn't look at him, nor did the cleaning woman who was letting herself into the public bar of the Waterlily. She too had a scarf swathing the lower half of her face. Arthur entered the mews as All Souls' clock struck eight.

Someone had left a newspaper, last evening's, on top of a dustbin in the mews. He picked it up and tucked it under his arm so that anyone who saw him would think he had been out to buy it. But no one saw him. Li-li's curtains were drawn. He crept upstairs through the sleeping house. On the top landing, resting against his door, was the orange laundry bag. At some point Li-li had brought that bag up the stairs. Had she knocked on his door? And if she had, would she have assumed he was asleep? Or had she left it downstairs, and had Anthony Johnson, the only other occupant of the house, been responsible for bringing it here? There was no way of knowing. If Anthony Johnson were awake now light would show from his window on to the court, for Room 2 was dark in winter till nine. But there was no cross-barred cast of light to be seen on the green stone. Snow whirled down the well, flying against the cellar door and streaming down it as rivulets of water.

Arthur cut up his handkerchief and flushed the pieces down the lavatory. He washed his scarf and, pulling it out from the lining, washed too the pocket of his overcoat. Then, and only then, did he dare look at his face in the mirror.

His eye socket was the colour of meat that has lain exposed, a dark, glazed red, and the lid was almost closed. And his lip was split, a cut running up unevenly at the centre join of the upper lip. He looked quite different, this wasn't his face, not his this sore, bulbous mouth. Would it scar? It didn't seem bad enough to need stitching. He washed it carefully with warm water and antiseptic. It couldn't be stitched. Every casualty department in every hospital in London would be alerted to watch for a man coming in with a wounded mouth.

He mustn't show himself at all. At any cost, he must remain here, hidden, until his lip and his eye healed. It was hours since he had eaten or drunk anything, hours since he had slept, but he knew he could no more sleep than he could eat a crumb of bread. He drank some water and gagged on it, its coldness burning his throat.

Shrouded by the nightdress frills of the net curtains, he crouched at the window. If the police did a house-to-house search he would be lost. He watched people go by, expecting always to see the piranha face of Inspector Glass. The church bells rang for morning service and a few elderly women went by, carrying Prayer Books, on their way to All Souls'. At lunchtime he put on the television, and the last item in a news bulletin told him, as only this high authority could really tell him, what he had done and where he stood.

"A man was attacked last night in a car park near Kenbourne Lane tube station in West London . . ." And there, on the screen, was the car park overhung by the ramparts of the Taj Mahal. Arthur trembled, clenching his hands. He half expected to see himself emerge from behind a row of cars, caught by those cameras like a stalked animal. "From the circumstances of the attack, police believe his assailant mistook him for a woman and are speculating as to whether the attacker could be the same man who, for a quarter of a century, has been known by the name of the Kenbourne Killer. A massive hunt in the area has so far been unsuccessful . . ."

Arthur switched off the set. He went once more into the bathroom and looked in the mirror at the face of the Kenbourne

Killer. Never, in the past, when he had thought of the things he had done, had he ever really considered that title and that role as belonging to him. But the television had told him so, it was so. Those marks had been put upon his face so that he and the world should know it. Looking at his face made him cry so he went back to his window where the nets veiled his face. The television remained off, blank, though an early Rogers-Astaire film was showing, until five when there was more news.

An Identikit picture appeared on the screen, a hard, cold face, sharply lined, vicious, elderly. The subject had a hare lip and a blind eye. Was that how he, so spruce and handsome, had looked to the boy with the Citroën? He felt faint and dizzy when the boy himself appeared and seemed to stare penetratingly into his own eyes. The boy put a hand up to that deceiving hair and smiled a little proudly.

"Well, I reckon this guy thought I was a girl, you know, on account of me being skinny and having long hair."

The interviewer addressed him with earnest approval. "Would you be able to identify him, Mr. Harrison?"

"Sure, I would. Anyway, I knocked his face about a bit, didn't I? Anyone'd be able to identify him, not just me."

And now Inspector Glass himself. Arthur shivered because his enemies were being ranged before him through this medium, once so friendly, once the purveyor of his second best delight.

The lips curled back and the great teeth showed. "You can take it as certain that the police won't rest until we've got this chap and put him out of harm's way. It's only a matter of time. But I'd like to tell the public that this man is highly dangerous, and if anyone has the slightest suspicion of his identity, if he or she feel they're only going on what you might call intuition, they must call this number at once."

The telephone number burned in white letters on a black ground. And the voice of Inspector Glass, the voice of a devourer of men, came heavy and grim.

"At any time of the day or night *you* can call this number. And if you hesitate, remember that next time it could be you or your wife or your mother or your daughter."

The diesel rattle of a taxi called Arthur back to the window. Li-li came out of the house carrying two suitcases. There was another gone who might see his face and not hesitate. Snow had begun to fall again through the bitter cold darkness. He watched her get into the taxi.

And now he was alone in the house with Anthony Johnson.

22

That Sunday it was nearly noon before Anthony got up. Room 2 was icy and he had to use powdered milk in his tea because he had run out of fresh. The courtyard was wet, although it wasn't raining, and the triangle of sky had the yellowish-grey look snow clouds give.

It was so dark that he had to keep the lamp on all day. He sat under it, leafing through the draft of his thesis, wondering if it was any good, but into his concentration, or what passed for concentration, fragmented images of Helen kept breaking. He found himself recalling conversations they had had in the past, reading duplicity into phrases of hers that had once seemed beautifully sincere. And this obsession displaced everything else. He sat staring dully at the pink and green translucent shade that swayed with a slow, gentle rhythm in the draught from the window-frame crack, hypnotised by it, subdued into apathy. Soon after five, when he had heard Li-li leave, he put on his coat and set off for Winter's.

The relief barman from the Waterlily was in the shop, and he and Winter were talking about the police activity of the night before. Anthony had forgotten all about it. Now, waiting to be served, he learned its nature.

"Young fellow of nineteen, student at Radclyffe College. What I say is, if they will get themselves up like girls, they're asking for it. Not that he didn't stand up for himself. Bashed the fellow's face up something shocking. You see the news?"

The barman nodded. "Funny thing, I got a black eye myself

last week. All above board, got it at my judo. But if it wasn't better I wouldn't fancy showing myself on the street."

"You didn't get a cut lip as well, though, did you? Mind you, that'd be a turn-up for the books, all the locals finding out the Kenbourne Killer'd been serving them their booze." Winter laughed. He turned to Anthony. "And what can I do for you, sir?"

"Just a pint of milk, please."

"Homogenised, Jersey, or silver top?"

Anthony took the silver top. As he was closing the door behind him he heard them say something about his hair and prowling stranglers who couldn't tell the boys from the girls, and who could blame them? He went past the lighted windows of the Waterlily, for only drunks and potential pick-ups go into pubs on their own in the evenings. The snow had settled in little drifts between the cobbles of Oriel Mews, where there was no light or heat to melt it. It floated thinly over Trinity Road, making a thinner, webbier curtain over the draped nets at Arthur Johnson's window behind which Anthony thought he could vaguely make out a watcher.

Room 2 had grown cold again in his absence. He kicked on the electric fire, drank some milk straight out of the bottle. It was so cold it made his teeth chatter. He crouched over the fire, and into his mind came a clear and sweet vision of Helen as she had been in the summer, running along the platform at Temple Meads to meet his train when he came to her from York. He felt, closing his eyes, her hands reach up to hold his shoulders, her warm breath from her parted lips on his lips. And he felt real pain, a shaft of pain in his left side, as if he had been kicked where his heart was.

Then he lay face downwards on the bed, hating himself for his weakness, wondering how he would get through the time ahead, the long and cold winter of isolation with only Arthur Johnson for company.

Upstairs, on the landing, the telephone began to ring.

~~~~~~~~~

Arthur heard the phone but didn't answer it. The only people who were likely to receive phone calls had gone away. He went into the bedroom and looked again at his face. Impossible to consider going to work tomorrow. The phone had stopped ringing. He looked out of the window down to the court below. Anthony Johnson's light was on, and Arthur wondered why he hadn't answered the phone.

There was plenty of food in his fridge, including the Sunday joint he hadn't been able to face and couldn't face now. The food he had would last him for days. He managed to swallow a small piece of bread and butter. Then he looked at his face again, this time in the bathroom mirror. While he was wondering if ice would ease the swelling, if anyone would believe him if he said he had cut himself shaving—and, presumably, also knocked his eye with the razor—the phone started ringing again. He opened his front door and emerged on to the dark landing. Obscurely he felt that, whoever this might be phoning, it would be safer were he to answer it himself.

He lifted the receiver and Stanley Caspian's voice said, "That you, Arthur? About time too. I buzzed you five minutes ago."

Light flooded him suddenly from the hall below. He turned, covering his mouth with his left hand, and called in a muffled voice, "It's all right, it's Mr. Caspian for me."

Anthony Johnson said, "O.K." and went back into Room 2. Arthur wished the light would go out. He hunched over the phone.

"Listen, Arthur, I've got a chap coming to have a dekko at Flat 1 tomorrow around five. Can you let him in?"

"I'm not well," Arthur said, sick with panic. "I've got a—a virus infection. I shan't be going to work and I can't let anyone in. I'm going to have the day in bed."

"My God, I suppose you can get out of your poxy bed just to open the front door?"

"No, I can't," Arthur said shrilly. "I'm ill. I should be in bed now."

"Charming. After all I've done for you, Arthur, that's a bit thick. I suppose I'll have to fix it a bit earlier with this chap and come myself."

"I'm sorry. I'm not well. I have to go and lie down."

Stanley didn't answer but crashed down the receiver. Arthur stumbled up to his own door. It was almost closed. A slight draught, a tiny push, and he would have been locked out. He who never never neglected such precautions had forgotten to drop the latch. Shivering at the thought of what might have happened, he went into the bathroom to contemplate his lip and his eye. Tears began to course down his face, stinging the bruised flesh.

~~~~~~~~~~~

The second time the phone rang Anthony got off his bed to answer it. But the hopes he had had, hopes that were against all reason, were dissipated by the voice calling from the landing, "It's Mr. Caspian for me."

Because the voice sounded thick and strange, Anthony, who in his disappointment would otherwise simply have drifted back into Room 2, glanced up at the figure on the landing. Arthur Johnson was covering his mouth with his left hand, and he turned away quickly, huddling over the phone, but not before Anthony had noticed one of his eyes was swollen and half-closed. The phone conversation went on for a few moments, Arthur Johnson protesting that he was ill, but from a virus infection, not some sort of facial injury. Anthony closed the door. He sat on the bed. An hour before he would have given a lot for some subject to come overpoweringly into his mind and crowd Helen out of it. But this? Did he want this and could he cope with it?

A series of images now. A man, evidently nervous, paranoid, repressed, saying, "You are the *other* Johnson, I have been here for twenty years." In the cellar a shop window model with a rent in her neck. Fire burning that figure, and that very night, the night of November 5 . . . Anthony looked out of the window and up to that other window two floors above. No light showed, though that was Arthur Johnson's bedroom and he had said he was ill and ought to be in bed. Perhaps he was, in the dark. Anthony went out into the street and looked up. There was light up there, orange light turning the draped muslin stuff to gold, and behind that shimmering stuff a light flickering movement.

He went quickly indoors and up the two flights of stairs. He had thought of no excuse for knocking on Arthur Johnson's door, but excuses seemed base and dishonest. Besides, once he had seen, he would need no excuse. But there was no answer to his knock, no answer when he knocked again, and that told him as much as if the damaged face had presented itself to him, six inches from his own. To knock again, to insist, would be a cruelty that revolted him, for in the silence he fancied he could sense a concentrated breath-held terror behind that door.

He knew now. He would have laughed at himself if this had been a laughing matter, for the irony was that he who was writing a thesis on psychopathy, who knew all about psychopaths, had lived three months in the same house as a psychopath and not known it. So, of course, he must go to the police. Knew? Did he? Well, he was sure, certain. When we say that, Helen had once said, we always mean we are not quite sure, not quite certain. He shivered in the hot, fuggy yet draughty room. It had been a shock. Presently he began looking through his books, finding Arthur Johnson or aspects of him in every case history, finding what he well knew already, that if hardly anything is known of the causes of psychopathy, even less has been discovered of ways to cure it. Forever a prison for the criminally insane then, forever incarceration, helplessly inflicted and helplessly borne. But he would go to the police in the morning . . .

At last he undressed and got into bed. The triangle of sky was a smoky red scudded with black flakes of snow. He found it impossible to sleep and wondered if the man upstairs, lying in bed some twenty feet above him, also lay sleepless under his far greater weight of care.

At eight-thirty in the morning Arthur phoned Mr. Grainger at home. He wouldn't be coming in, would have to take at least three days off. While he was on the phone he heard Anthony Johnson go into the bathroom, but the man didn't come to the foot of the stairs. Why had he knocked on his door last night? To borrow something, to get change for the phone? Still fresh with him, still aching in his bruised ribs, was the terror those repeated knocks had brought. But nothing would have made him let Anthony Johnson in to see his face. For hours he had hunched over the window ledge, intermittently leaving his post to look at his face, to listen by the door for Anthony Johnson to phone the police, watching for Anthony Johnson to go out and fetch the police. By midnight, when nothing had happened and the little court had gone dark, he had lain down, spent but sleepless.

~~~~~~~~~

The last of four lectures by a distinguished visiting criminologist was to be given at the college that morning. Anthony had attended them all, been rather disappointed that they were more elementary than he had hoped, and now took notes abstractedly. He was tired and uneasy.

Still he hesitated to go to the police, although he had noted where the nearest station was, having passed its tall portals, its blue lamp, on his way to college on the K.12. One o'clock came and he was in the canteen, vacillating still, nauseated at the idea of betraying a man who had done him no injury. He seldom had much to say to the students. They were all younger than he and they seemed to him not much more than children. But now a girl who had sat next to him in the lecture room brought her tray to his table and pointed out to him a long-haired boy who was holding court at the far end of the room, surrounded by avid listeners.

"That's Philip Harrison."

"Philip Harrison?"

"The guy who was attacked in the car park on Saturday."

Anthony didn't look at him. He looked at the young girls who were his audience, one of whom was distressingly like Helen. If that girl had been in the car park she wouldn't be here now, listening with innocent relish. She would be dead. He had only to go to the police station and tell them what he knew, so little that he knew, so tenuous as it was, yet so true a pointer. Dully, he pushed away his plate. He had eaten nothing. A great weariness overcame him and he wanted nothing so much as to lie down and sleep. He remembered how, once in the summer, he and Helen had lain in each other's arms in a field in the West Country and for an hour he had slept with her hair against his cheek and the scent coming to him of seeded grass and wild parsley.

Since then, it seemed, he had never slept so sweetly as during that hour. But the summer was past, in every sense, and the sweet hours of sleep. He got his coat, walked down the long hall, through the swing doors, out into the snow.

The police station was perhaps ten minutes' walk away. The college grounds were empty and barren as if the cold had shaved all vegetation away but for the clipped turf and swept up all people like so much litter. There was no one in the grounds but himself and a girl whom he could see in the extreme distance coming in by the main gates. He walked towards her and she towards him down the long gravel drive.

And now he began collecting together his knowledge and suspicions of Arthur Johnson for a coherent statement to the police. But he was distracted by the sight of the approaching girl. By now he ought to be used to the deceptions practised on him by his eyes and his mind. He wasn't going to catch his breath this time because a strange girl walked like Helen, moved her head like Helen, and now that she came nearer could be seen to have Helen's crisp, golden hair. He trudged on, looking down at the gravel, refusing any longer to contemplate the girl who was now only some twenty or thirty yards from him.

But, in spite of himself, he was aware that she had stopped. She had stopped and was staring straight at him. He swallowed hard and his heart thudded. They stared at each other across the cold bare expanse. As he saw her lift her arms and open them, and as she began to run towards him, calling his name, "Tony, Tony!" he too ran towards her with open arms.

Her mouth was cold on his mouth but her body was warm. As he held her he knew he hadn't been warm like this for weeks. The warmth was wonderful and the feel of her, but he was afraid to look at her face.

"Helen," he said, "is it really you?"

23

They sat on a bench on College Green, not feeling the cold. Anthony held her face in his hands. He smoothed back a lock of hair that had fallen over her forehead, relearning the look and the feel of her. "I don't believe it," he said. "I really can't yet believe it."

"I know. I felt like that."

"You won't go away? I mean, you won't say in a minute that you've got a train to catch or anything like that?"

"I've nowhere *to* go. I've burned my boats. Tony, let's eat. I'm hungry, I'm starving. You know I always want to eat when I'm happy."

The Grand Duke was crowded. They went into a café that was humble and clean and almost empty.

"I don't know whether to sit opposite you or next to you. One way I can look, the other way I can touch you."

"Look at me," she said. "I want to look at you."

She sat down and fixed her eyes on his face. She reached across the table and took his hand. They held hands on the cloth, hers covering his. "Tony, it's all right now, it will always be all right *now*, but why didn't you answer my letters?"

"Because you told me not to. You told me never to write to you."

"Not my last three. I begged you to write to me at the museum. Didn't you *get* them?"

He shook his head. "Since the end of October I've only had one letter from you and that was the one where you told me you never wanted to see me again."

She drew back, then leaned forward, clutching his hand. "I never wrote such a thing!"

"Someone did. Roger?"

"I don't know. I don't—well, it's possible, but . . . I wrote and told you I was leaving him and coming to you. But how could I come when you didn't answer? I was crazy with misery. Roger went to Scotland and I waited at home alone night after night for you to phone."

"I phoned," he said, "on the last Wednesday of November."

"By then I'd gone to my mother's. I'd got a fortnight's holiday owing to me and I went to my mother because I couldn't bear being alone any more and being with Roger in Scotland would have been worse. I thought I'd never see you again."

Just as he had thought he would never again see her. But now he had no wish to solve the mystery. It paled into insignificance beside the joy of being with her.

"Helen," he said, "why are you here now?"

"But you know that," she said, surprised. "I'm here because you wrote to me."

"*That* letter? That stupid letter?"

"Was it? I never saw it. I only know you said you loved me in the first line of it, so I—I ran away!"

She leaned across the table and kissed him. The waitress gave a slight cough and, as they drew apart, placed their plates in front of them.

~~~~~~~~~~

"I went to work this morning, my first day back. As soon as I got in the phone rang and it was Roger. A letter had come for me with your name and address on the flap and he—he opened it."

"My name and address on the flap? But I . . ." He explained how he had enclosed his letter to her in one to Mrs. Pontifex.

"Oh, I see. We never meant to go there for Christmas this year. She must have copied your name and address from the letter to her and forwarded it. I don't know. I told you, I didn't see it. I went out before the post came. Roger was—he was *frightening* with rage. I've heard him in some rages, I've seen him, when he's threatened to kill me and himself, but I've never heard him like that. He just read that first line and then he sort of spat out, 'From your lover.' He said, 'You're to go downstairs and wait outside the building for me, Helen. If you're not there I'll come up, but you'd better be there unless you want a public scene. I shan't flinch from telling anyone in that building what you are.'

"He said he'd be there in the car in five minutes, Tony. I knew it couldn't take him more than five minutes and I was terrified of what he'd do. I grabbed my coat and my handbag and I rushed out and down the stairs. I remember calling out I'd had bad news and had to go.

"When I got into the street I was afraid to wait there even for a second. I crossed the road and ran down a side street, and then a taxi came and I said, 'Temple Meads!' because I knew I must go to London and you. You loved me, you'd said you did, so everything was all right at last.

"I didn't bother to queue up for a ticket. I could hear an announcer saying, 'The train standing at platform two is the nine fifty-one for London, calling at Bath, Swindon and Reading.' It was nine-fifty then and I jumped on that train. I had to buy a ticket when the man came round and it took all the money I'd got but for five pence. I hadn't got a chequebook or a bank card or anything. Oh, Tony, I'm entirely skint, I've got just what I stand up in.

"When I got to Paddington I found a bus going to Kenbourne Vale Garage but I hadn't got enough money to get further than to Kensal Rise. So I walked the rest."

"You *walked?* Here from Kensal Rise?"

She smiled at his dismay. "Out in the cold, cold snow and without any money. All I needed was a baby in my arms. I went into a news agent's and looked up the route in a guide. I was going to go to Trinity Road but then I thought you might be here. So I came here and here I am." Her eyes were bright, the pupils mirrors in which, at last, he could see his own face reflected. "Are you pleased?" she said.

"Helen, I was half dead with misery and loneliness and you ask me if I'm *pleased?*"

"I only wish," she said, "that I'd seen your letter. I don't suppose I ever shall now and I'd waited so long for it. Can you remember what you wrote?"

"No," he lied. "No, only that it was nonsense. You had the only good bit in the first line."

She sighed, but it was a sigh of happiness. "Tony, what are we going to do? Where shall we go?"

"Who cares? Somewhere, anywhere. We shall survive. Right now we'll go to Trinity Road."

As he spoke the name he remembered. It was nearly three o'clock and he had delayed long enough. He put an arm round her shoulders, helped her to her feet. "Come along, my love, we're going to Trinity Road, but we'll take in an errand I have to do on the way."

~~~~~~~~~~

Behind the curtains Arthur had sat all day, breaking his vigil every half-hour or so to examine his face in the bathroom mirror. Now, at three o'clock, he saw Stanley Caspian's car draw up and park in front of one of the houses on the odd-numbered side. A man was coming to view Flat 1, and in a moment this man and Stanley would come into the house. Arthur watched the car but he could only see Stanley in it, sitting in the driving seat, his bulk and the bikini doll impeding further view. Perhaps he had brought the man with him or perhaps he was simply waiting for the new tenant to arrive for his appointment. Arthur went back to the bathroom. Already, so early, the winter light was beginning to fade. If Stanley did happen to call on him, if he had to show his face, perhaps those dreadful marks would pass unnoticed. . . .

As he came out of the bathroom his doorbell rang. The sound reverberated through Arthur's body and he gave a tremendous start. He stood stock still in the hall. It was evident what had happened. Stanley had forgotten his key. Let him go home and fetch it then. The bell rang again, insistently, and Arthur could picture Stanley's fat finger pressed hard and impatiently on the push. He forced himself to go back into the living room and look out of the window. Stanley's car was empty. At any rate, it must be he. No police cars anywhere, no parked vehicles but Stanley's and a couple of vans and a grey convertible. Another long ring fetched him back into the hall. He must answer it, for it would look odder if he didn't. But he was supposed to be ill and must give the appearance of having been got out of bed. Quickly, though he was shaking, he slipped off his jacket and took his dressing gown from the hook behind the bedroom door. A handkerchief to his face, he let himself out of the flat and went downstairs.

Outlined behind the red and green glass panels was the shape of a heavy, thick-set man. It must be Stanley. Arthur stood behind the door and pulled it open towards him. The man marched in, looked to the right, then to the left where Arthur stood, took the edge of the door in both hands and slammed it shut as violently as Jonathan Dean had slammed it in the past.

He was youngish, dark, and he was in the grip of an emotion greater even than Arthur's fear. Arthur didn't know what this emotion was, but he knew a policeman wouldn't look like this, stand trembling and wide-eyed and wild like this. Because the hall was shadowy, lit with a misty redness and greenness, he took the handkerchief away from his face and stepped back.

"Is your name Johnson?"

"Yes," said Arthur.

"A. Johnson?"

Arthur nodded, mystified, for the man peered at him incredulously. "My God, an old man! It's unbelievable." But he did believe and when he said hoarsely, "Where is she?" Arthur also knew and believed.

Once it would have been threatening, dreadful. Now it was only a relief. "You want the other Johnson," Arthur said coldly and stiffly. "Sit down and wait for him if you like. It's no business of mine."

"The *other* Johnson? Don't give me that." His eyes travelled over Arthur's dressing gown. He clenched his fists and said again, "*Where is she?*"

Arthur turned his back and climbed the stairs. He must get to his flat, shut himself in and pray that Stanley would soon come to turn this intruder out before violence drew the police. And now, realising what could happen, he ran up the second flight to push open his own front door. A cry of dread broke from him.

He had no key, hadn't dropped the latch, and the door had closed fast behind him.

He stood shaking, his back to the door, his hands creeping to shield his face. Out here what chance had he when Stanley came with the new tenant, when trouble broke out between Anthony Johnson and H's husband? And now the man had reached the head of the stairs and was facing him. Arthur looked into the barrel of a small gun—a pistol or a revolver, he didn't know which. Television hadn't taught him that.

"Open that door!"

"I can't. I've no key. I've left my key inside."

"My wife is in there. Open that door or I'll shoot the lock off. I'll give you thirty seconds to open that door."

His front door shattered, swinging on its hinges, would be worse than his front door locked against him. Arthur, who had moved aside when he saw the gun, brought his gaze first to the smooth circle of metal surrounding the keyhole, then, with greater dread, to the smooth metal cylinder pointed at that keyhole. A voice like a woman's, a victim's, screamed out of him.

"I can't! I tell you I can't. Go away, get out, leave me alone!" And he threw his body, arms upraised, against the door.

Something struck him a violent blow on his back, on the lower left side. The pain was unimaginable. He thought it was his heart, a heart attack, for he felt the pain long long before he heard the report as of a bursting firework, and heard too his own cry and that of another, aghast and terrified. Arthur fell backwards, his hands clutching his ribs. The pain roared in a red stream out of his mouth.

Heavily he rolled down the stairs, blood wrapping his body like a long scarlet scarf. The momentum flung him against Brian Kotowsky's door and there he felt the last beat of his heart in blood against his hand.